# THE LONG ROAD TO GRACE

*Robert Lewis Wilson*

ISBN: 0692617299
ISBN 13: 9780692617298
Library of Congress Control Number: 2016906088
Robert Lewis Wilson, Austin, TX

# PREFACE

One year ago I was given my freedom, or at least that's how I now I refer to it. But on that day, five years and another embarrassing divorce later, it didn't feel like freedom at all.

Last year, I had a choice. I could mull around in self-pity, or I could get on my knees and ask God to change me. Not to be taller or thinner, but to really change me, to change me within. A divorce is devastating to one's self-esteem and mine was at an all-time low. (*Author's note: Those of you that never suffered from self-esteem issues can stop reading here. You won't understand what it's like to sabotage your own success, love, fatherhood, friendship or anything else that you want because you've convinced yourself you're too tall, too ugly, too fat, too stupid, too whateverthehell you've been told all your life.*) After my divorce, the only way I was going to be able to love myself was if I could see myself as God does, as his child, loved regardless of my actions. That still blows my mind!

Listen, we're are all works in progress and we never get it figured out. But at the end of the day, only two people know the truth about you: you and God. And if God loves you the way you are, then why don't you? There is no "I love you, but" with God. There shouldn't be for ourselves either.

Since my divorce, I have tried so many new things. I've written this book, I've travelled to another country twice, I'm speaking another language, I've spent more time with my family and friends, and even fell in love (albeit in a completely different way), all in spite of me. I'm living each day like it is my last. I say yes to the things I use to always say no to. And it all started with a commitment to see myself as God sees me and that, my friends, is true freedom.

# ACKNOWLEDGMENTS

First, I must thank God for never leaving me, even though several times I turned my back on him. I thank him for his countless blessings in my life, healing me when I was broken, and showing me how to see myself as he sees me.

I thank my parents for instilling in me right from wrong. They gave me life lessons on how to treat other people and ask for forgiveness when we failed them. They taught me how to love, to cry, to laugh and above all, that God was to be the top priority in my life.

I am deeply thankful to Pat for the years of putting me through school and raising our wonderful children. I could not have gotten this far without your love and support.

And to my children, Robby, Eric and Megan, while at times it doesn't seem like it, you are my life. I can't thank you enough for still being in my life, especially after so many years of me being a fool. I am proud of you love you more than you'll know.

To Barb, my dear friend. Thank you for your encouragement, your support and your dedication. One can go a lifetime and never share what we've shared. You've seen me crazy, you've seen my tears, heard my laughter and put me to bed when I couldn't get there myself. Thank you for always being there.

I can't end it without saying thank you to special people that have entered my life and made an impact – Pastor Randal and Kevin. Your friendship and prayers have kept me alive. Karen M., thank you for all those late night talks on the phone while I was writing this book. Your input and your friendship is priceless! My buddy Nick in South Africa. Good times and bad times came upon us like a tidal wave but we managed our way through it.

I apologize for those that I left out. If you're in my life after all of these years, thank you. You've made a positive impact on me whether you know it or not.

And finally:

Claribel, mi reina. Eres mi gracia, mi regalo de Dios. Gracias por estar en mi vida.

# THE JOURNEY

*Enter through the narrow gate. For wide is the gate and
broad is the road that leads to destruction, and many
enter through it. But small is the gate and narrow is the
road that leads to life and only a few find it.*

*—Matthew 7:13–14*

I guess I've lived long enough now to understand that everyone
has a story. Just like people, no two stories are the same. There
are similarities, but no two are exactly alike. This is my story of my
journey through life.

I agree with the scripture regarding the roads. There are two
roads to travel as you go through life. The narrow road is light, and
the broad road is dark. Unless we are born into a family of felons
and miscreants, we start our life walking on the road of light. We
attend church, go to Vacation Bible School, and learn about God.
But for so many of us, circumstances both within our control and
beyond as well as people we let into our lives attract us to the broad
and dark road. While so many people choose this road, it is not the
easiest road to walk. There are bumps, hills, ruts, and potholes on

this road. There are no road signs or markers to help us along it. We keep wandering aimlessly down that broad road and through that wide gate to destruction. I've known people on the narrow path. They, too, have had bumps, hills, ruts, and potholes, but they always seem to have some beacon of light, or direction, to guide them on their journey. Whether by reading the word of God or through their involvement in a church, I believe it is their faith in God that leads them.

I spent some thirty-odd years of my life serpentining both roads. I would walk that narrow and light-filled road with direction and the prospect of a good life, with hopes of passing through the narrow gate. Other times, I ran to that broad road. I was pulled off the narrow path by the attraction of all the things the world could offer me: sex, drugs, alcohol, and the ability to have all my needs met instantly. The life of instant gratification of the flesh was everything I hoped it would be and more. Little did I know the scripture would prove right. It was a road to destruction. Self-destruction.

This is my story.

# CHAPTER 1

# IT'S ALIVE

*When a woman is giving birth, she has sorrow because her hour has come, but when she has delivered the baby, she no longer remembers the anguish, for joy that a human being has been born into the world.*

*—John 16:21*

My name is Ramsey Carter Jackson. Yep, I'm the kid you made fun of all through school for having three last names. Momma's maiden name was Ramsey, and Daddy's mother's maiden name was Carter. Blue-blood Texans name their kids after family. Somehow, my parents must have thought they were blue-blood Texans. Hell, the only thing blue about us was our eyes and our collars. So I got made fun of plenty. It didn't help that I grew really fast. That just fueled the jokes of being the extratall, extraskinny kid with three last names. And just like everyone else I know, I didn't ask to be born.

Two women had the most impact in my life. My momma was from a strong Christian background, and my paternal grandmother was a real saint. So many times I watched them fall to their knees and pray for someone. And they always let me know they were praying for me. As a little kid, I went to Vacation Bible School because my momma made me. I also went to church with Granny when I visited her each summer. Granny had the "gift" of speaking in tongues. To me it sounded like she was conjuring some kind of spirit. To be honest, it scared the crap out of me, so religion didn't really catch on with me early on. However, as you can imagine, I did get mighty familiar with the Bible. But when Daddy got religion, I really got to know it.

Momma was a meek woman, and it was only after she died that I realized how strong she was. But one thing about it, my momma loved me, and without a doubt I was her favorite, regardless of what my little brother said. Momma always told me about the joy she felt when I was born. But it was my welts and cuts on my back and legs that Momma tended to that brought us closer together than her and my three siblings. She would put ice and medicine on my skin and tell me how much she and my daddy really loved me. I don't think I ever believed her while I was at home. I loved my momma, but I never could figure out why she would let my old man beat on me. I also became the one most like my momma. I always got picked on for having a woman's heart, and I was too weak.

My old man drank a lot. I found out later that his old man drank a lot, and so did *his* old man, and so on. Daddy was a military man, but I swear he should have been a tightrope walker, because he had some kind of balance. He was the only dad I knew who could beat you with a belt in one hand and a beer in the other and would never spill a drop. Later, when he got religion, he traded out the beer for a Bible and could still make his point with the belt. He reminded me of a painting I once saw of John Brown, the abolitionist who led a raid on Harpers Ferry. The painting depicts

John Brown with a Bible in one hand and a rifle in the other, larger than life, standing on the dead slave owners. Just seeing that picture and imagining my old man as John Brown was enough to keep me in line.

I answered the altar call at twelve or thirteen at a Nazarene summer camp in the Texas Hill Country. There was a young preacher and an awesome band that led us in singing old hymns under the stars, under an open tabernacle. The praise was so strong that night that we called on the Holy Spirit, and It filled that entire place and each one of us teens and preteens, brought us to our knees, and filled our hearts with joy and our eyes with tears. I wish God would have taken me then. I would have been guaranteed a spot in heaven.

When I got back from the camp, I really believed I was going to stay strong as a Christian. I got involved in church, sang in the choir and had an occasional solo. I had a passion for God, and I believed one day I would make my momma proud and become a preacher.

But as most new Christians find out, it's easier said than done to live in such a dark world and try to live your life for Christ. So as hard as I tried to live the right life, that same year I started to live a life in two worlds. Daddy saw me as a pussy of a kid with no backbone, spouting off "yes, sirs" and "no, sirs" without even needing to be reminded. I was a well-groomed, well-mannered son with no direction. But I knew I was going to get beat for something, so I started doing things without Daddy knowing it.

With Daddy drinking so much, it was no surprise that by the time I was twelve, I had already started my own legacy of drinking a lot. I kept a salad-dressing bottle full of a mixture of Jim Beam, Bacardi rum, and Smirnoff vodka in my locker at my junior high school. I also became quite an entrepreneur. I sold shots of liquor out of my locker for two dollars. Then I moved on to a better business venture. My big brother always had nudie magazines, and I sold pages of those to the kids around my locker. Don't get me wrong; I wasn't popular by any means. I was just a good business-man. Then I began stealing. Small things at first, like comic books, candy, and gum. But later I stole beer and liquor and passed coun-terfeit one-dollar bills that were made to look like twenties. I also began starting fires. I set our house on fire twice and the woods near our house once. I loved building pipe bombs and blowing the shit out of things.

I never hurt people. It wasn't my intention, but, man, I sure liked fucking stuff up. Sure, I got caught for some things, and the old man tore my ass up, but the things I didn't get caught for made up for the other senseless, rage-fueled beatings. I always gave him a reason to beat me, whether he knew it or not. That's why I didn't grow up hating my old man. And all during this time, I still lived the Christian life on Sunday mornings. I think I truly believed God was so busy with other people whose sins were worse than mine that he gave me a pass for my behavior.

Some people saw me as a really good boy. I was a nice man. I was a momma's boy. I was the guy your mom wanted you to marry. I was an educated man who always had a good job and made a good living. Even in my professional life, I was respected by my peers. I was always a good provider. I was sometimes a really good Christian man. I tithed, went to Sunday school, sang the hymns out loud, served on the church board, and even collected the of-fering. It was my faith and belief in God, even in the worst of times, that kept me alive. Again, I do wonder, though, why God bothered to keep me alive.

But I was also a very bad boy. I've been an arsonist, a drug dealer, a whore monger, a pimp, a gambler, an adulterer, a coun-terfeiter, a bully, a liar, a cheat, a blasphemer, a home wrecker, an idol worshiper, a drunk, a sex addict, a drug addict, and a lot more than I care to remember. I once tried to kill a person with my bare hands. I've had knives and guns pulled on me. I was on the losing end of a Russian roulette game, and only an intervention by God and a friend's quick hand kept the gun from going off. I've been in handcuffs for fun and for restraint. I've done so much damage to the people I've met, and to some that I haven't, that only God, the offended, and I know the truth. And I'm praying that at least one in that trinity has forgiven me.

The life I have lived is responsible for failed marriages, ruined friendships and relationships, financial failure, and utter hopelessness. It has caused lost sleep, night terrors, and night sweats. In the middle of the night, I have been awakened to my own laughing, crying, and blood-curdling screams. I've had both suicidal thoughts and murderous thoughts. I've spent so many nights on my knees begging God for a way out and then asking Him to please take my life. The pain and suffering of my self-imposed misery, self-deprecating behavior, and self-loathing was just unbearable. If I didn't love me, who could? Because all I ever wanted from the time I came out of my mother's womb was love.

# CHAPTER 2
# ENTER GIRLS AND WOMEN

*Now the works of the flesh are evident: sexual immorality,*
*impurity, sensuality.*

*—Galatians 5:19*

O ne thing that stayed constant throughout my life was my love
for girls and then women. I kissed my first girl at the age of
seven. Sure it was a peck on the lips, but it felt really good, and I
knew I wanted to do it again. But the real change in my life came
when I was twelve, just a couple of days after I became a Christian at
that Nazarene summer camp. There was an eighteen-year-old neighbor girl who lived down the street. I was selling vegetable and flower
seeds door to door. I had responded to an advertisement that was in
the back of a comic book, and a business venture was spawned.

The girl, Dawn, said her parents weren't home and invited me
in. She had on a tank top with no bra underneath and a pair of
cutoff blue-jean shorts (later referred to as Daisy Dukes). To this
point, I didn't have much experience seeing breasts, restrained

or otherwise. Sure, I sometimes looked at the Sears-catalog bra section and the *National Geographic* magazines with the natives of South America or Africa. What boys my age didn't? She told me she would be right back with the money for the seeds.

I was standing in the hall when she called me back to her room. I slowly walked back, but the door was closed. She said to come in. I did, and she was lying on her bed, naked to the world and me. I felt my face flush and turned to walk out. She told me to turn around and stand by the bed. I really didn't know why she wanted me in there, but she acted angry, and I went back. I looked at her body, and for the first time, I saw a woman's breasts. She was a skinny girl with short, black hair. Her breasts were smaller than the ones I had seen in the magazines. She told me to give her my hand. I did, and she put my hand on her left breast. I tried to pull away. I had no idea what was going on, but I was getting warm, and something was happening to me in my crotch area. She told me to hold her breast and massage it. I squeezed it, but I guess I was doing it wrong. She seemed really frustrated. So she opened her legs, and I remember seeing a lot of hair. She was still holding my hand, and she told me to stick my finger out. I did. She took my hand and guided it inside her. It was wet and really warm. There was a look on her face that really scared me. I tried to pull away, but she told me she would tell my daddy. She knew he would tear my ass up. Tears began rolling down my face as she took my hand and made it go in and out a couple of times.

She said to never tell anyone, and I never did. She said she didn't have any money, but she would make sure her mom bought seeds if I came back later. I didn't. I walked home, crying the entire way. I'm not sure why. I guess I felt somewhat violated, but at the same time, I'd liked it. Something happened to me that day. It was almost like the church camp but in a bad way. Things happened in my body and my mind that I didn't understand. Little did I realize that my life was changed forever because of this one day.

So, my first French kiss was at fourteen. I had no idea why any-one would want to taste the inside of another person's mouth, but once I did it, I couldn't stop. Gone forever was the innocent peck on the lips.

After that, I moved on to bigger things. My first experience at sexual intercourse was when I was sixteen, and it was with a twenty-year-old woman. My God, she was beautiful, wonderful, and pa-tient. I worked in a grocery store, and she came in at least three times a week and always came through my checkout line.

One day she asked, "Is this all you do—is work?"

I laughed and told her no and that I also went to high school. She laughed it off, and that was it. She kept coming through my line, and we kind of flirted with each other, but I was damned shy.

One day she asked what time I got off work. It was a Wednesday night, so I was getting off early since I had to go to bed. She said she would come by and see me when I got off. Sure enough, she showed up at eight o'clock and was waiting for me outside. My parents were at church, so she told me to get in her car and we would go for a drive. We went to a country-western dance club. I told her I had to get home before my parents did, and she assured me I would.

We went in, and since I was already six foot eight and the drink-ing age was eighteen, I hardly ever had my ID checked. So I bought us a couple of beers, and we got a table. We danced to quite a few songs and went back to the table for a rest. I was real shy, and I think I cracked a few jokes. I didn't know what else to do. It got quiet for a minute, and I looked into her brown eyes, tempting me, taunting me, flashing beacons of I dare you. That's when it hap-pened. I leaned in and kissed her. I immediately backed up and said, "I'm really sorry."

She said, "Don't worry about it. I liked it. You can do it again if you want."

I moved back in, and we kissed at the table for a good minute or so. She said she was ready to go. We got out to her car, and I opened her door to let her in. But she didn't get in. She turned and hugged me, and we started kissing again. This time really passionately. I could feel things happening in places that I wasn't sure what to do with. She took me home, and my parents were already home, so we kissed in my driveway. I got out, thanked her for a good time, and went in. When I got inside, the old man was already waiting for me.

"You're running a bit late aren't you, son?" he asked.

I told him I had to get a ride from someone else. I was so glad he didn't smell the three beers on my breath. I went into my room and immediately masturbated.

One Saturday night after work, around midnight, she was outside waiting for me when I got off. We got in my car, which I had just bought from my parents. We were just sitting in the parking lot when she suggested we drive around. We drove for a bit until I got close to a construction site. She told me to pull in there and turn off the lights. I did. We started kissing again, and she lay down in the front seat. We fumbled around, getting our pants down and her shirt up. I was anticipating it and became real excited. This was the day I'd been waiting for.

But then it happened. I went soft. Yep, the little train that couldn't. I became upset. I couldn't believe this happened. I knew I liked girls and not boys. There was no mistaking that. She held me there in the car while I lay on top of her. She told me to relax and we could try again another time. She kissed me and soothed me until I calmed down. I figured that was my last chance because there was never going to be another chance. I took her back to her car and, again, went home and masturbated. To my extreme satisfaction, there were no equipment malfunctions this time.

The next night she came in, and we flirted a bit at my cash register. Close to closing time, she was again outside waiting for me. We drove back to the same spot. This time, I wasted no time in getting down to business. We kissed for a short time, and I mounted her in the front seat of my Oldsmobile! And there it was. With all of the vulgarity of a sailor's tongue, a few short thrusts from my youthful hips, and a loving and willing instructor, I was now welcomed into manhood.

# CHAPTER 3

# AND NOW I AM A MAN

*When I was a child, I spoke like a child, I reasoned like a child. When I became a man, I gave up childish ways.*

*—1 Corinthians 13:11*

What was flirting turned to puppy love and then to sex, and what was now sex began to form a deeper love. I loved this woman with all my heart. She was nurturing, loving, and respectful, and I knew she loved me. But as much as a man I thought I was, I was still a teenager—a human being whose brain has not developed to its full size and whose pleasure center (and hence self-centeredness) is the only part of the brain that works properly. My brain became one that equated sex with love. A girl at high school started paying close attention to me. I started paying attention to her. And worse yet we went out a couple of times while I was still steady with the other. Eventually, and so horribly immature of me, I broke it off with the woman I loved to be with the other. On my seventeenth birthday of all days! Up until then I had never seen a woman cry. Even my mother didn't cry when my dad beat us kids. My God, my love!

A day I will always regret. She cried even into the next day. She was crying when I called to check up on her. For almost all of my life, I had never been loved, respected, and cared for more by anyone else. I guess to this day I still love her with all my heart.

This new girl was something. A pretty maiden for sure, and I loved the way she walked. We started off our dating in bed. We didn't waste any time getting to that point, and it was something we were good at. Youthful sex by the way. We had no imagination at all. Suffice it to say for some of us, missionary will be all that we know. We were in love I guess. We both had an abusive parent to deal with, so it was a relationship of convenience, and it seemed like the right thing at the time.

One night, she had some news. She hadn't gotten her period and was worried. I had no clue what to do. So I went in and talked to her psycho mother and told her I would do the right thing. I felt like, when I left the house, I had a gun pointed at me about to go off at any time. It was the strangest feeling I ever had. Later I found out her mother said she was going to kill me if her daughter wound up pregnant. Lucky for me, I guess, a couple days later, my girl had her period. But the fact that all adults involved knew we were having sex only fast-forwarded the relationship. So we graduated high school and got married right away.

We moved out of town and away from our controlling parents. We moved to South Texas, and I started working in the oil field as a derrick hand. I worked six days a week, and my wife spent our money seven days a week. The work was tough, nasty, and extremely dirty, but I loved doing it. I was really a good derrick hand because I was tall enough to work the tall pipes and had the flexibility to work the short stuff. It was a hard bunch of people to work with. In my three years working there, twenty-two men from our crew had come and gone from that rig, and I was the only one who hadn't been to jail or prison. It was here among these guys where I learned to smoke a lot of weed and drink even more. One night, Mike, one of the hands from the rig and a crazy bastard that I ran around with, shared a joint with me. I got seriously wasted and to the point of being scared. He laughed uncontrollably and told me I had just smoked weed laced with angel dust. I had no idea what that was, but I do know I was so wasted I set off a ball of primer cord attached to a blasting cap in my front yard, and it blew a huge hole in my yard; the explosion broke out the front windows in my house. Then I drove my pickup to the end of the street and T-boned a ditch. I woke the next day in my own bed, looking at a bloodstained pillow, but my front teeth were still in the steering wheel.

After that episode the marriage pretty much turned to shit. We had a couple of kids in three years, and my wife was sleeping with one of my workmates. So after a ton of drama, we got a divorce, and I wound up with a child-support bill. And to make matters worse, I moved back home and looked up my first love. Yep, she was already married with a kid. Ah, you can never go back, can you? After Dad read me the house rules and a couple of chapters of Proverbs from the Bible while I was in a drunken stupor at his table, I left and moved in with a friend of a friend.

Before I walked out the door, Dad called me back in and said, "Look, son, I know you know about the birds and the bees, so I'm not going to help you with that. But I am going to read you something that you had better learn now, or it will bring you a lifetime of misery." He opened his Bible, and he began to read the following verse aloud:

**Warning against the Adulterous Woman**
My son, keep my words
    and store up my commands within you.
Keep my commands and you will live;
    guard my teachings as the apple of your eye.
Bind them on your fingers;
    write them on the tablet of your heart.

Say to wisdom, "You are my sister,"
    and to insight, "You are my relative."
They will keep you from the adulterous woman,
    from the wayward woman with her seductive words.
At the window of my house
    I looked down through the lattice.
I saw among the simple,
    I noticed among the young men,
    a youth who had no sense.
He was going down the street near her corner,
    walking along in the direction of her house
at twilight, as the day was fading,
    as the dark of night set in.
Then out came a woman to meet him,
    dressed like a prostitute and with crafty intent.
(She is unruly and defiant,
    her feet never stay at home;
now in the street, now in the squares,
    at every corner she lurks.)
She took hold of him and kissed him
    and with a brazen face she said:
"Today I fulfilled my vows,
    and I have food from my fellowship offering at home.
So I came out to meet you;
    I looked for you and have found you!
I have covered my bed
    with colored linens from Egypt.
I have perfumed my bed
    with myrrh, aloes and cinnamon.
Come, let's drink deeply of love till morning;
    let's enjoy ourselves with love!
My husband is not at home;
    he has gone on a long journey.

He took his purse filled with money
    and will not be home till full moon."
With persuasive words she led him astray;
    she seduced him with her smooth talk.
All at once he followed her
    like an ox going to the slaughter,
like a deer stepping into a noose
till an arrow pierces his liver,
like a bird darting into a snare,
    little knowing it will cost him his life.
Now then, my sons, listen to me;
    pay attention to what I say.
Do not let your heart turn to her ways
    or stray into her paths.
Many are the victims she has brought down;
    her slain are a mighty throng.
Her house is a highway to the grave,
    leading down to the chambers of death.

—Proverbs 7

My old man knew where I was headed. He must have seen it in me at an early age. I wish I hadn't been so drunk and so stupid. I wish I would have listened to my dad. Instead, I shook his hand and said sarcastically, "Thanks for that, Dad. I'm sure I'll find it useful.

"He looked at me with utter contempt and pointed his finger in my face. "Get out, and go get your shit together. I'll be praying for you, but I feel Satan already has his hand on your heart."

I turned and left. I didn't come home for a long time.

# CHAPTER 4

# THE BAD BEGINNING

*The acts of the flesh are obvious; sexual immorality,
impurity and debauchery.*

*—Galatians 5:19*

After my divorce I wasn't dating. To be honest I was afraid of women. One night, one of my high-school mates, Ezra, gave me a call. Ezra was one of the black students who had been bused from the other side of town when they closed their high school and decided to integrate all of us in the city. I had suffered a pretty bad beating from a group of black kids on the first day of school. Ezra had come to my aid and stopped them from pretty much kicking my head in. He and I got to be friends after that, even though I was from the kicker crowd and he was from the bused-in black crowd. The way I figured it, anyone who stood up for me was a friend of mine. The reason he called me was that he heard I was single again and wanted to see if I'd like to go get a couple of beers. He knew my ex, so we talked about the marriage and how it fell apart.

He told me he never understood us dating, much less getting married. We moved on in conversation, and he asked if I had been dating. I pretty much confessed I was sworn off that for a while. He said, "Let's go for a drive."

We got into his car and headed toward the "bad" side of town. I had never been there. It was a myth that any white kids caught over there would be stripped naked, beaten, and then driven back across town. I didn't want to bust the myth. I was shocked at what I saw. Along this one street, there were prostitutes working both sides of the street. We pulled alongside a couple of really pretty black girls. Ezra rolled his window down.

One of the girls leaned in and said, "Hey, baby, what chu doin' with that good-lookin' piece of vanilla wafer there?"

Ezra laughed, but I was nervous. "We're looking for a date," he said.

I quizzically looked over at Ezra.

"Just play along, Ram."

The other lady looked in and said, "Well, you boys are just in luck because we were just talking about how we needed to find us a date."

Ezra negotiated a price and a location and away we went. "I'm about to get you laid, Ram!" he yelled.

"No offense, Ezra, but I've never been with a black girl," I said.

I must have really sounded like a wimp to him. But he just said, "You ain't gonna say that after tonight."

We met them at a hotel. They had already gotten a room. We walked in, and I don't even think we exchanged names. There was one bed, and I must have looked puzzled because one of the girls said, "We ain't fuckin' on no floor."

So we all got undressed. I and my girl were on one side of the bed, and Ezra and his on the other. We got straight to work. At one point when we were in midstroke, I looked over at Ezra, he looked over at me, and we just grinned. We were fucking two prostitutes in the same bed at the same time. That was just the beginning of a crazy life.

No man starts out to be a bad boy. We all had to have a teacher. Mine was a woman—Ellie. Without a doubt, she was the craziest woman I ever met. I was fresh meat from the divorce, and she worked at a store that I delivered snack foods to. She worked in the meat-market section as a meat wrapper. Now I see the irony of it all. I would walk by her, and she would always say, "Hey, tall guy. When are you going to ask me out on a date?"

I would blush and lie. "Pretty soon."

To be honest, after my divorce at age twenty-two, I had no game whatsoever. Hell, I couldn't even talk to a woman without stammering, blushing, and almost passing out. But Ellie, she was persistent. One day, I walked by, smiled, and said hello.

She said, "Wait! I've got something for you."

I wanted to run away.

She wrote her number down on a piece of paper and pressed it into my hand. She said, "Call me tonight, tall guy."

I said I would, and I looked at the paper. It read, "Call me! Ellie—515-555-6667." I was scared to death. I figured she was out of my league for sure. She was hot, but at the same time, she had that little bit of "fight, fuck, or piss for distance" attitude that redneck girls have. Yeah, she was all cowgirl, all right. She always wore tight jeans, a big barrel-racing belt buckle, and boots. I never saw her top as she always wore a white smock. But I could see she didn't have much in the way of breasts.

I went home, changed my clothes, and lifted weights. Even as a twenty-two-year-old, I was real skinny and was trying to build bulk for my six-feet-nine-inch frame. I thought about Ellie the whole time. So I showered, got cleaned up, and considered going to the local country dance hall. Instead, I grabbed the number and went to the phone. One ring and she answered hello in a damned sexy voice.

"Ellie?" I asked.

She chuckled. "Is this that tall guy?"

I could only muster to say in a weak voice, "Yeah, it's Ramsey."

After minimal small talk, she finally she said, "I need your help. I'm about to take a bath, and I need you to wash my back."

I actually hyperventilated.

"Here's my address now. Hurry before the water gets cold. The door is unlocked," she said as she rushed me off the phone.

She lived about thirty minutes away, but I know I made it in twenty. I gently knocked on the door, and she screamed, "I said it's unlocked!"

I walked in and locked the door behind me. I started walking toward where I heard water splashing. The bathroom door was open, and there she was in the tub. There wasn't much in the way of suds left, and I could see her small breasts in the soapy water.

"Come sit here," she said as she patted the side of the tub.

I walked over, sat, and looked into her blue eyes. I finally saw her. She was a blond-haired, blue-eyed, five-feet-three-inch, 110-pound sexy woman. Her frame was slender, her breasts were small, and she was a natural blonde.

"What took you so long?" she asked, her voice barely audible, making it sexy as hell. She got up on her knees in the tub, put her arms around me, and kissed me full on the mouth.

I was frozen. I didn't even kiss back. She forced my lips open with her tongue, and we began kissing—crazy, passionate, open-mouthed, biting, tongue-sucking kissing. My heart was pumping almost out of my chest.

"Stand up," she ordered me.

I stood up with her arms still around me. She made a kind of a jump move and came out of the tub, dripping water but with her arms still around my neck and her legs wrapped around me. So I was standing there fully clothed, holding a wet woman, try-ing to imagine what was next. We resumed kissing, and she began grinding her groin against my pants. I was about to bust. She told me to turn around and walk to the bedroom. I walked her in there. We were kissing, panting, and moaning, and I fell on the bed with her still in my arms.

I was undoing my pants when she yelled, "Me first!" I'm sure the look on my face was of shock if not panic. She was already naked. I moved back toward her, and she grabbed my hair and my ears, looked into my eyes, and said, "I said, me first." Because I wasn't real experienced, I didn't know what she meant. She pushed my head down toward her crotch, and it finally dawned on me what she wanted. "That's it, tall guy," she said approvingly as I fumbled my way through the experience. She stopped me. "Not there. Here." And she gently moved me around and instructed me. Finally, she arched her back and screamed, "Daddy! Oh, Daddy!"

Honest to God, I wanted to run out of that freak show. It scared the hell out of me. What I did have working was gone now. I was lost at this point.

She patted the bed next to her and said, "Your turn, tall guy. Lie down." She stood up and took off my boots and my jeans. I sat up to take off my shirt. She pushed me hard with both hands on my chest and said, "I said, lie the fuck down!"

Now it was at this time I realized the television was on, and lo and behold, it was the *PTL Club*. Praise the Lord for sure! No, seriously, I'm not being blasphemous here. So as she started going down on me, I was wondering, *What the hell did I get mixed up in?* I peeked around her and saw Tammy Faye in all of that clown makeup, praying for some soul. I was thinking, *Please pray for me, Tammy, so I can get out of here alive.*

Ellie did things to me that night I had only read about in *Penthouse Forum*. I did things to Ellie that I had never heard another man or woman mention, much less read about it. With her direction that night and for weeks to come, she taught me how to be a bad boy. I screwed it up. As would soon be a pattern for most of my life, I fell in love with her. Yes, this was the first time I confused sex and love. And of course, any mention of God after this point was basically when His name was used in vain.

Ellie continued to educate me in all that there was to know about sexual pleasure. I have no idea where she learned it, but it was quite fun being her student. A couple of months later, she called for me to come over so she could show me her new purchase. I went in her bedroom, and there was a monstrous, king-sized water bed.

"Come on, let's play," she said.

I answered, "We might as well break it in."

She smiled and said, "Sorry, tall guy. Already broke in."

You see, smart people who understand comments like that walk away. I passed it off for being a used water bed.

"Huh?" I asked.

"I fucked the water-bed guy," she answered without even blinking. "He was going to charge me to put it together. I figured why not get it done for free."

I guess I should have realized right then and there that this would be a pattern in her life. But you see, love had a way of clouding my thinking. I was able to get past what she had just told me, because I was the one who was going to "fix" her. I told her how hurt I was and that I didn't understand why she did it. To this day, I don't remember her answer, but I do remember breaking down and crying.

"It's not that big of a deal, honey. It didn't mean anything," she explained.

First lesson in fucking a stranger doesn't mean anything. Damn, so young and learning so much.

So we patched up that episode, and our relationship continued. One night I spent the night at her house and was sound asleep when I woke to the sound of someone banging on the door.

"Ellie! Open the fucking door, Ellie!"

In my sales job, I often collected large amounts of cash and carried a pistol with me everywhere I went. I had it lying on the floor under the bed. Naked, I grabbed my pistol and made a beeline for the front door. I loudly inquired, "Who the fuck is pounding on my door?"

He yelled back, "It's Jeff! I need to see Ellie!" He pounded on the door again.

I looked at Ellie, who was so beautifully naked in the hall. I whispered, "Who's Jeff?"

"It's the water-bed guy," she whispered back like it was no big deal.

I cocked the hammer back on the pistol. "Did you hear that, Jeff? That's my three-fifty-seven Magnum getting ready to shoot a hole in this fucking door if you don't leave."

It got real quiet. No, I mean the crickets weren't even chirping. I was shaking so bad. I don't know what had me shaking more—the anger, the adrenaline from almost shooting someone, or the disbelief of what she just told me. I heard Jeff's car start, went back to the bedroom window, and watched him drive off. A few minutes later, I left as well. I told her we were done. She was crazy, and I wanted no part of that shit. Stay gone. Another lesson I should have learned.

She constantly called me, and I constantly hung up. I started a new job as a lineman for a power company and began working out of town quite a bit, so I didn't have to put up with her phone calls. There were always messages. I just deleted them. All was good. I had met a cute college girl out of town because, after being with Ellie, I now had the confidence to start going out. Sue was her name, and we started going out dancing a bit and usually wound up in my hotel room. I liked her, but I was pretty screwed up between my divorce and Ellie. So any chance of a real relationship was nonexistent.

I had moved in with my older brother after Ellie. One night he and I went to the country dance club. We met these college girls, and they wound up joining our table. We had a blast. I set my sights on a really pretty girl from Dallas. She was blond and pretty, but a bit on the curvy side. But, man, did she have big breasts! That was a whole new item in the toy box since no woman I had been with from the start was well endowed.

My brother was talking with a brunette in the bunch. We wound up going home together. Celia was the blonde's name. I'll never forget it. We spent three hours in my bed, making out. Fully clothed! We kissed, we touched, and we did everything but take our clothes off. Finally, she succumbed to the pressure of my hands on the outside of her pants. We got naked, and I remembered the lessons Ellie had taught me. I have to say, to that point in my lifetime, ecstasy exclamations had only consisted in moaning and an "Oh, Daddy" or two. Celia laughed. What the hell? Yes, she laughed, but I assure you the laughter did not match the look on her face. When I was done, I rolled over and lit a cigarette.

"What was that?" she asked.

I grinned and said, "I had lessons." That was all I could think of to say.

We saw each other a couple of times after that. Again, it was usually just a movie or dancing and winding up in my bed. One night she called and said she and her friends were going to the dance hall. I told her a friend and I would meet them there. We got there, and I saw a new girl in the bunch.

# CHAPTER 5

# ENTER THE BAD BOY

*For such people are not serving our Lord Christ, but their own appetites. By smooth talk and flattery, they deceive the minds of naïve people.*

*—Romans 16:18*

She was a Yankee. I could tell by the way she talked. Turns out she was from upstate New York. She stood out in the crowd of blond friends of hers. She had long brown hair, brown eyes, and a smile that melted me. Every time I would look at this girl, Celia would see me, and I would look away. She was getting pretty irritated, so I pulled Celia onto the dance floor to keep her calmed down. While she was in my arms, she would look up and try and make eye contact, but I was already trying to figure out how to be with her friend, so I would look away. We stayed on the dance floor for a bit, and she excused herself to the ladies room.

I walked over to her friend and introduced myself. Her name was Linda. I asked her if she knew that "Linda" was Spanish for "pretty." She laughed and said she had never heard that. I asked her to dance. I remember the smell of her hair and the way it felt when it brushed my face as she put her head on my shoulder. She had curves in the right places, and we danced slow and easy. I loved the way my hands felt on her waist, and I pulled her close.

She said, "Please don't. Celia is my best friend."

I said, "Celia doesn't have to know. Come closer." I pulled her in, and my knee was in her crotch as we continued to dance.

"Please, I want to, but I can't."

I looked over and saw Celia looking at us. She was fidgeting and was quite disturbed about what was happening on the dance floor. I let go of Linda as soon as the dance was over and walked over to Celia.

"You're an asshole. You do know that, right?" she said to me with venom. "And you, Linda. What the hell are you doing?"

Linda looked at me and then down to the floor. "We were just dancing," she replied quietly.

It was obvious to me that Celia was the leader of this pack. But I wanted Linda. Of course I did.

"Let's go!" said Celia.

"Hang on!" I exclaimed.

She told Linda and the other girls, "I'm going outside and leaving in five minutes. If you're not there, I'm leaving without you." She looked at me. "Don't you ever call me again!" She stormed out.

Linda looked at me and shook her head.

"Hold on," I said. "Please let me call you."

She looked surprised. "Are you serious? No way! She'll kill me!"

Again, I said, "Celia doesn't have to know. Please, your number?"

She rolled her eyes and dug a pen out of her purse. She wrote her number on my hand. "I hope this washes off, and you don't call."

I think it was about one o'clock in the morning when I got home. I looked at my hand and wrote Linda's number on a piece of paper. I called the number.

"I knew you were going to call me!" she answered.

My only comeback was from psychiatry 101: "How do you feel about that, Linda?"

"You know Celia hates you, right?"

I answered, "I'm sure she does, but what about you, Linda?"

She answered with what I know now was a damned foreshadowing answer: "Let's just see how it goes from here."

Later that week I took Linda to dinner. We had a really great time getting to know each other. I really liked her, and I think the feeling was mutual. We went for a long walk by the city lake. We began making out on a park bench. It got pretty heated. Damn, she could kiss. After a bit, we realized we needed to go somewhere quick, so we went to her apartment. We made love twice that night. I say that because it was the beginning of something special. Hell, a few weeks later, I even took her to meet my parents.

One night I cooked dinner for her at my brother's house, where I was staying. It was in the country and had a long dirt road to get from the highway to the house. Right about the time we were about to eat, the phone rang. I thought about letting it go to the message machine. Too late—I picked it up.

"What are you doing?" It was Ellie.

I looked at Linda, and my face must have been full of panic. "I'm about ready to go dancing," I lied.

"Which place?" she kept on.

"Does it matter?" I shot back. Then I told her the dance hall that was the farthest from where we were.

"OK, I'll see you there," she said and hung up.

Linda and I were in the bedroom, lying in bed after making love. I was sitting up on one elbow, watching her as she lay naked in my bed. She was just looking up at me, smiling. Yes, all was good in the world. I was falling in love again. I really can't tell you if it was because of the sex. I guess it didn't hurt. I didn't have curtains on my window since we were in the country. I looked out and saw headlights speeding up the gravel road, leaving behind a cloud of dust. The lights came closer, and I realized it was Ellie's pickup truck slamming to a stop and sliding at least ten feet in the gravel. She left her headlights on, and I could see her storming as she walked in front of her headlights, heading for my front door.

"Get dressed!" I yelled at Linda.

"Who is it?" She looked pretty scared.

"Get dressed!"

"Open this door, motherfucker!" Ellie yelled. She pounded on the door at least ten times. "I know you've got a girl in there! Open this fucking door."

I had just made it to the kitchen when that crazy bitch kicked in my door.

Linda was slow behind me, and you could tell, she was confused and scared. "Who is she?" asked Linda.

"It's my ex," I said.

Ellie just stormed past me and had almost grabbed Linda's hair when I grabbed her, pinning her arms against her side. I held her up in the air. She was wriggling, trying to get loose, kicking me, and screaming at Linda, "Bitch! Get the fuck out!"

"Calm down, Ellie, or I'm going to call the fucking cops!" I yelled.

"Did you fuck her? I hope it was worth it!" she was still screaming.

I was squeezing her harder and wasn't letting her go, which only made her madder. Linda was trying to sidestep behind me as I had Ellie in front of me.

"Are you calm?" I asked as Ellie was starting to go limp.

"No, I'm not fucking calm. Get out of here, bitch! I'm not going to calm down until she's gone."

I said in a calm voice, "Now, Ellie, let's talk this out, and then we can figure out what to do next."

She stopped resisting, and I let go and stood her on the floor, still holding her by her wrist. Ellie was staring at Linda. Poor

Linda—she was shaking, and tears were in her eyes. I couldn't trust turning Ellie loose so I could go comfort Linda.

"Ramsey, tell her to leave," Linda finally said.

Ellie jumped toward her again, and I pulled her right back against me. "Now stop being stupid!"

It got really quiet. Linda was looking at me, her eyes begging me to tell Ellie to leave. I was restraining Ellie, and Ellie was glaring at Linda.

"I'm sorry, Linda," I said. "Please leave. I'm really sorry."

Linda knew all along how this would end. Somehow I knew it too. Man, what a weak piece of shit I was.

Linda started crying as she walked by me into the bedroom to get her things. She walked back by and was bawling now. "I hate you! Celia tried to warn me! Don't you ever call me again!"

There it was. The reason I can't be in love. I was starting this pattern of using women.

"Ha-ha, bitch! You lose!" yelled Ellie.

I was still holding Ellie's wrist and flung her to the ground. "Don't you fucking move from there until I tell you!"

I followed Linda out and tried to turn her.

"Don't you ever touch me again!"

She was still bawling and got into her car. She started it, and I was standing in front of it. I truly believe I asked God to please have her run me over. Ellie would have, but not Linda. She backed up and drove away without looking at me one more time. The one that got away and the one I kept—for now. I couldn't even be a good bad boy.

As my decision and fate would have it, I moved in with Ellie. We continued to fuck like bunnies and fight like pit bulls. Not really about anything, but the damage was done. I was still working out of town the Sue, my girlfriend from out of town, and we actually became a couple while I was there. I was the only guy on the crew with a steady out of town and constantly caught shit about it from the guys. Somehow, I reconciled what I was doing was fine. I even think Ellie knew, but she didn't bring it up.

Of course, I already suspected her of having sex with the entire neighborhood. One night when I came home, there was a note: *Don't be here when I get back. I'm on a date.* I ran through the house, destroying everything in my path. I broke a kitchen knife off in the water bed, and water flowed everywhere. I took my shotgun and sat in a chair and waited. And waited. In walked Ellie, by herself. She saw my truck outside and knew not to bring in her fuck mate. She saw me sitting there with the shotgun. The only thing she asked me was what had happened to the bed. I stood up and put the shotgun in a corner and walked toward her. She kicked me right in the groin. I was sent off balance for a bit, and then she slapped me upside both sides of my head with each hand. I grabbed her by her throat and picked her up off the ground. I watched her trying to struggle. Trying to breath. I don't remember much, except there was a calm about the entire room. *I could hear my grandmother and my mother both praying for me to let go.* I let her go, and she fell to the floor. I had my back turned to her and was walking toward the door. I only heard the *boom*! She shot a hole in the ceiling right above my head. The roar of the gun had made me temporarily deaf. And mad as hell. I walked back to her, grabbed the gun from her, and body slammed her back to the ground. I walked outside and put the gun in an outdoor closet, up in the attic part. I climbed up on the hood of her truck, kicked in her windshield, and kicked in the grill.

I was just about to leave, and as I turned the corner, a sheriff deputy had just gotten out of his car and was aiming his handgun at me.

"Get down! Get down now!"

I got down and lay flat on my stomach immediately, and he ran over and jammed his knee in my neck. "Where's the gun?"

I could only answer, "What gun?"

He said, "Someone called in that shots were fired." He cuffed me and picked me up, and we walked back toward the house. He leaned me against her truck. I admired my handiwork of damage to it while I watched the deputy walk back to Ellie.

Ellie was there waiting to tell her story. And tell it she did. Her neck was already bruising. I figured all of the freedoms I had enjoyed to this point in time were about to be taken away from me. *I hear my grandmother and my mother both praying for them to let me go.* Ellie called the deputy aside and talked to him privately. They were standing pretty close to each other, whispering. I couldn't believe it.

I yelled, "What, are you fucking her too?"

He quietly walked over as if to say something in my ear, but instead he hit me in the solar plexus and completely had me on the ground, still in handcuffs, trying to get my breath. "You might want to keep quiet for a bit while we sort this out."

He walked back over to her, and for a few minutes, they talked. As I lay on the ground, I looked over and strained to hear what they were saying.

He came back and lifted me up off the ground by my shirt. "She's not pressing charges. You need to get your stuff and get out. Oh, yeah, you need to give her a thousand dollars for the damages before you leave."

I couldn't believe it. "A thousand fucking dollars? This is bullshit, and you know it."

He walked back over and made a move again to get closer, to tell me something. I tensed, waiting for another blow. This time he said, "You're not focusing on the big picture. You're not going to jail."

So I loaded up my stuff (including the shotgun) and wrote her a check for $1,000. I had everything packed in my truck. "Can I leave now, Officer? If there's anything else, you're going to have to catch me."

The deputy just shook his head and said, "If that check doesn't clear, I'll make you wish I hadn't let you go."

I flipped him off and spun out as they watched me drive off.

I was going up the road leading out of the subdivision at seventy-five miles per hour in a thirty-five-miles-per-hour speed zone. There was a car approaching, and I hit a dip in the road just as I passed one of Texas's finest, a DPS patrol car. I felt the load of stuff in the back of my truck shift. I watched my mirror as he slammed on his brakes and turned on his lights. I thought about running. I really did. But something told me to pull over. I was already busted. I got out and waited, and he rolled up on my truck. His gun was already in his hand as he got out.

"Get on the fucking ground! Now! Do it!"

I stammered, "Dude, what's your problem. I was only speeding."

He quickly screamed again, "If I say it again, I'll shoot you where you stand."

This guy was pissed, and he was serious. I immediately hit the ground for the second time that night.

"What did you throw at me?" he asked.

"Huh? I didn't throw anything at you, Officer. I just left a fight and was driving out of here mad. The county guys just let me go."

He sarcastically answered, "Yeah, I was headed to that call. Have you been drinking?"

For the first time in I don't know how long, I could answer no to that question. "No, sir!"

"Are you taking drugs?"

"No, sir!"

He put me in cuffs and threw me into the back of his car. He secured my truck and called for a wrecker.

"What are you charging me with, Officer?" I asked.

"You're being detained for suspicion of DWI. We're going to the station to do a Breathalyzer test," he answered.

So I went to the jailhouse, took the stupid test, and passed with flying colors. Turns out, an album flew out of my stereo as the load shifted when I hit the dip in the road, and it hit the officer's windshield. So I paid $150 for my impounded truck, $1,000 to Ellie, and $300 for a speeding ticket. I should have stayed gone the first time. What a bad boy.

*Give thanks in all circumstances, for this is God's will for you in Christ Jesus.*

—1 Thessalonians 5:18

# CHAPTER 6
# JUST FOR THE HELL OF IT

*People will be lovers of themselves, lovers of money,*
*boastful, proud, abusive, disobedient to their parents,*
*ungrateful, unholy.*

*—2 Timothy 3:2*

After I left Ellie, I moved in with a couple of roommates. I was pretty down one day and was lying on the couch in a funk. One of my roommates, Ray, came by and kicked the couch.

"Get the fuck up!"

I lay there looking up at him. "Fuck you, Ray. Leave me alone."

He had a lit cigarette in his hand and flicked it at me, hitting me in the chest and sending lit embers everywhere. "Leave me alone." He mocked in a whiney voice. I wheeled my legs around to get up, and he beat me to it, put me in a headlock, and brought me down, slamming my face into the carpet. He lay on top of my head and back, pinning me to the ground, still holding me in a headlock. I thought he was going to choke me out.

"You need to get over that bitch!" he yelled. "I'm going to tell you how you're going to do it and then let you up, OK?"

I was quiet for a moment and then said, "OK?" I was pissed, but I agreed.

"We are going to throw the biggest party we've ever had," he started. "And you, Ram, are going to get laid. You got it? The best way to get over someone is to get under someone."

Again, I reluctantly agreed. We needed money, and quite a bit. First we made money the easy way. One of things we enjoyed was varmint hunting in Central Texas. We would go out at nights and spotlight raccoons, possums, fox, and bobcat and kill them for their fur. It was the beginning of the '80s, and people still wore fur. So when we needed extra money, we hunted. That week, we snorted meth for a couple of nights in a row, hunted all night, and had enough furs to sell to pay for a party. We went on a spending spree and bought everything we needed. We bought weed, crystal meth, coke, pills, X, and a shitload of booze.

We started the party on a Sunday night. Ray had an old girl-friend who was now a lesbian, and she brought the whole lipstick crowd over. These weren't the plaid-shirt guy-looking girls. Oh, hell no. They were all beauties. There were people jammed up everywhere. The phone rang, and I figured it was someone saying he or she was on the way over. I answered it without thinking about how loud the music was. I could barely hear the other end.

"Ramsey?"

I said, "Yeah, this is him. Who is this?"

It was Ellie. Of course it was. I think it showed on my face.

Ray looked at me. "Hang up the phone!"

I took it into my bedroom. "What do you want, Ellie?" I asked.

"I just wanted to see if you're all right," she replied.

My heart was pounding. I started to cry. I don't think I even know why.

She said, "I still love you."

Love? I did a fast rewind in my mind, trying to find where in the hell in that crazy relationship love ever resided. It was an addiction, but it wasn't love. The door opened. I figured Ray was going to come in and snatch the phone out of my hand. It was Roxy. Beautiful, lipstick-lesbian Roxanne! She had long brown hair, red lipstick, long red fingernails, blue eyes, and a body like a model. She had on a light-blue tube top and white summer pants. Funny thing, I still remember, she was barefoot and had red toenail polish that matched her fingernails. I was sitting on the bed, and she walked toward me. I still had Ellie on the phone.

"Ramsey? Are you still there, hon?" Ellie quizzed.

I had mostly stopped crying and was looking at Roxy. She came to me and rubbed her fingers through my hair. She took the phone out of my hand, hung up, and tossed it on the floor.

"Lie back," she ordered.

I lay on the bed. She sat on top of me, leaned down, and began kissing me on the mouth, her long brown hair sprawled all around me. She sat up and pulled off her tube top, exposing her ample breasts. She smiled and looked down at me, my face stained with dry tears. She bent down and began kissing my face, gently licking my dry tears away.

She softly spoke, "It's OK now."

I wanted to start crying again. She was so gentle and loving. Stop. Not loving. She was so gentle and nurturing. There was a knock on the door.

"Is everything all right in there?" Ray asked.

Roxy started gently sucking on my neck.

I answered, "Right as rain, boss."

He responded, "All right then. Let's fucking party!"

I could hear the crowd in the other room all yell in unison. There's something about a noisy room full of people outside your door that just makes the sex you're having a little more intense. We quickly and sloppily got undressed, and Roxy resumed her place on top of me. A little more kissing and heavy petting and we began to have sex. She leaned over and was staring at my face as she began grinding me, clawing my chest with her long nails. She began moaning and grunting, and with each grind, she got a little louder. I held her hips and began thrusting. We finished together, and she went limp and lay on top of me with me still inside her. I was getting those feelings in my stomach. I could love this woman.

What the fuck, man! Stop that shit. You just fucked. That's it. No flowers, no candy, no date. S-E-X, man.

She rolled off. "All better now?" She laughed.

"Yep, all better." I grinned.

We got our clothes on and went back to the party. That party lasted four days with people coming in and out all day long. Even the neighbors were all there, except for the pretty redhead next door with the two teenage daughters. She didn't like us much, but I helped her around the house at times, so she didn't complain about the noise or call the cops. I saw Roxy a couple of times after the party, but we just hugged, said hello, and moved on. I only heard from Ellie one more time after this. That night with Roxy was what I needed to get back on track.

# CHAPTER 7

# LIFE IN THE SLOW LANE

*Put to death, therefore, whatever belongs to your earthly nature, sexual immorality, impurity, lust, evil desires and greed, which is idolatry.*

*—Colossians 3:5*

The next six months were a haze filled with drugs, booze, and prostitutes. I don't remember much and can't believe I held a job. At the end of the six months, Ray had a steady girlfriend and moved out. He introduced me to one of his high-school buddies, J. J., and he moved in a couple weeks later. He was a pretty heavy stoner but mainly kept to himself in his room. So with him not being very social, the parties stopped. I was getting burned out, and I felt like I was ready for a change anyway. That change happened one day while I was in a grocery store. I ran into a woman I had met about the time I met Ellie. She hadn't changed much. She was a pretty redhead and had a bubbly personality. Her name was Christine, but she went by Chrissy. She was married the first time I met her, but while we talked in the aisle in the store, she told me she had gotten a divorce about six months earlier. She made it a point to tell me she never had kids. She knew I was a bit rough around the edges, but she knew me mostly as a good guy. We wrapped up the conversation, and she gave me her number and said to call her sometime. I called her and set up a date for the next Saturday.

Saturday morning I got a call. It was Ellie. "Hey, Ram. I'm in town. Can I stop by?"

I couldn't imagine what she wanted, but my heart was already cold to her. I said it would be fine, but I was leaving later. She showed up about an hour later. I let her in, and we talked for a bit.

Finally, she said, "Can we go in the bedroom and just make out?"

She went from being a total psycho when I left her a few months ago to this sweet little kitten. We went in, making out lasted about five minutes, and then we got down to doing what we did best. Fuck. And fuck we did. There was no love in this. When I was done, I rolled off and lit a cigarette.

"How was it, Ram? Was it like it was before?" she asked.

Ah, shit. This was the opportunity I had been waiting for since we broke up. "I'll be honest, Ellie. It really wasn't all that," I said.

The waterworks started. I was with her a total of almost a year, and I never saw a tear in her eye, much less bawling. I told her it was time for her to go. I watched her walk off with tears in her eyes. I didn't even offer a hug as she was walking away. Good fucking riddance!

I went out with Chrissy that evening. We had a blast! It was almost like we were old souls who had known each other for a while. I took her back to her apartment and kissed her at the front door. She didn't invite me in, so I left it at that. I told her I would call her again. We went out a few times after that night with the same results. This one was different. No sex. We went to dinner and movies and just hung out and talked. We did some heavy petting, but I didn't push for anything further, and she wasn't inviting. We dated for about six weeks. I was still out of town, so there was mostly just getting to know each other by phone. After one of our dates, I went into her house. We went outside, had a beer, and smoked a joint. We started making out and found ourselves back in the house in bed. This was different. This was making love.

I had been starting to get sober lately, and getting to know her had changed something in me. I was ready to fall in love. And I did. We both did. After six months went by, I had finally given up the boozing and the drugs. I had an occasional beer and only smoked pot if we were at a party. One year later we moved in together. I decided to go to school, so I changed jobs and really started to get my shit together and make something of my life. I did well in my job and school. I hadn't been there very long, and I had my first promotion. The company allowed me to work an easier schedule so I could increase my hours in school. Things rolled along fine. We were both making a lot of money, and I was taking a crazy class load trying to graduate early. We still found time to travel all over the United States, hiking in the mountains and sunbathing on the beaches. We were one hell of a team. Then it happened. She was pregnant.

Neither of us wanted kids. My ex got my two kids, and I didn't get to see them very much because of my past drug and alcohol use. Chrissy and I never discussed having kids, so the subject came up. None of our siblings had kids either, so we were never around them. I was close to graduating, and she had moved up to an executive position. We tried to talk about her being pregnant. We just didn't. One afternoon, I came home from school to get dressed for work, and she was in bed. She was pretty lethargic and didn't get up. I asked if she was sick. She asked me to sit on the bed with her. Either I was in denial or I was just that stupid, but I didn't realize what she was going to tell me.

"I had an abortion this morning, Ramsey," she said weakly.

My face went flush, and I was sick to my stomach. I'm not sure why I reacted that way because we never talked about the pregnancy. I guess I wanted to be involved.

"Did you just decide to wake up this morning and get that done?" I asked. "Why couldn't you have included me? I would like to have been there for you."

She said, "I didn't want to upset you, so I asked my sister to take me."

I just stared ahead. I was numb, but I didn't really know why. I guess I'd never known anyone who'd had an abortion. And this was my kid that was aborted. I guess I felt betrayed. We didn't talk much for about a week, and then things kind of went back to normal.

Six months later I was a college graduate. I lasted that same six months with the company I worked for and finally quit. Too many changes in the company made my job no longer fun. I was recruited by a former coworker to a start-up company as part of the management team. Hell, yes. This degree already paid off, and I was moving up. More money meant we could buy a nice house and nice cars and live like we were supposed to. Maybe even think about getting married. And I loved my new workmates. All of that was great! The thing about my new workmates is they were all married, but they all partied hard. They partied during lunch, after work, and then on weekends. I started drinking again. A lot. I also had hurt my back, so I began taking Vicodin for the pain. Oh, tequila and Vicodin, the evil concoction. While at work I held it together, but at home I was becoming more withdrawn and unavailable. All of that was the beginning of the end.

# CHAPTER 8
# THE UNRAVELING

*But a man who commits adultery has no sense; whoever*
*does so destroys himself.*

*—Proverbs 6:32*

The company I worked for figured I needed an assistant. I talked to friends, and someone recommended a lady who would be perfect for the job. She was overqualified for an assistant, but she had a great attitude and a willingness to get the job done. I figured I needed someone like her to run things to help me keep my shit together at work.

Liz was a tall, skinny brunette with short, curly hair and a beautiful smile. She was a hippy chick—you know, one with her own style of fashion. But she was married with a kid, and I was in a serious relationship with Chrissy. As far as I was concerned, we were just workmates.

I went into work one Saturday to get some things done that I had let slip due to our shifting deadlines. I noticed Liz's car in the parking lot, so I figured she must be catching up as well. I said hello when I walked in, went and sat at my desk, and began typing up some report that was due on Monday.

A little while later, Liz walked into my office and asked if I needed anything. Not unusual, as sometimes when I was too busy to get out of my chair, she chased down some coffee for me. I did, in fact, need her to look over the report I just typed. I told her I would print it off in a few minutes and she could check it.

"Don't bother. I'll just read over your shoulder."

Most people prefer to read on paper, but I figured one less tree killed. She came up behind my chair, bent down—with her head to the left of my shoulder—and was looking at the screen. I could smell the Ivory soap from her body—she was that close. Her face was about eight inches away, and my heart started beating pretty fast. I looked over at her, and she looked at me. We held that gaze for what seemed like five minutes, although I know it was seconds.

I glanced quickly at the opening in the V neck of her white T-shirt revealing a braless set of small but perky breasts. I must have blushed because she just smiled and went back to reading the screen. I turned back to the screen as well. I looked back at her again, and this time she turned to me and came in a bit closer. I kissed her full on the lips and quickly pulled away.

"I'm sorry. I...I don't know—" I stammered.

"Shh, shh." She came in toward me again.

We began kissing passionately, ignoring everything that was wrong with what we were doing. She moved around in front of me as I rolled my chair away from my desk. She straddled me in my chair, and we continued to kiss as if we had held this back for years. She pulled off her T-shirt revealing what I had only caught a glimpse of. She had a beautiful body that motherhood had not harmed. We moved to the floor, removed our clothes, and made love.

Afterward, we lay on the floor, silent, but still holding each other. I don't know how long we stayed like that, but finally, I got dressed.

"So what now?" I asked, finally breaking the long silence.

"Why don't we just see where this goes?" Liz replied. I had already heard that before.

*Great*, I thought, *I'm going to catch bloody hell for this.* We finished our work, locked up, and left. Just like that, no kiss, no hug, nothing. I spent the rest of the weekend wondering what I just got myself into.

On Monday I came in, and Liz was already there. We smiled at each other, and I went on into my office. I had to meet a client later that afternoon, so I was preparing for the meeting. Liz walked into my office and asked if she could go to the client meeting and observe. Since she never had many opportunities to leave the office, I figured what the hell. I also decided it would be a good time to talk about what to do next.

It was a pretty silent trip to the client's office as we just exchanged the usual stuff about how the weekend went, her kid's baseball, and all that. We got in the car to leave, and she moved over from the passenger window to right in the middle, sitting right next to me.

"Do you mind?" she asked.

"No, I guess not."

Shit, what was I to say? No? I started driving, and we came to a red light. I looked over and smiled, and immediately our lips were back into action, kissing with a fury. Some ass honked behind me as I guess I got caught up and the light had changed.

All I could think of was where we could pull over and focus our attention. I spotted a neighborhood Little League park and pulled in out of street view. It wasn't baseball season, and since this was a park-and-ride parking place, there were other cars around. We started going at it like a couple of high-school kids making out, groping each other, and trying to figure out how we could make love in the car. We did with minor difficulty.

That's the way our relationship went for over two years—sneaky, self-serving, juvenile, hot, passionate sex. We were able to hide that relationship that long without either of us getting caught, getting hurt, or getting fired. I started working out and got into shape, quit the Vicodin, and boozed a whole lot less. It seemed like my relationship with Liz made my entire life a whole lot better. In my feeble mind, I thought that whatever this was, it would last forever. I even proposed to Chrissy, and we were planning a wedding later that year. Yes, I loved Chrissy, but was in love with Liz. Or at least I was in love with the idea of Liz and what we were doing. I thought of Liz every moment I was without her, and she said the same about me. We would call each other when we went to the grocery store or ran errands or whenever we were alone. I didn't pick up the phone if I knew it wasn't safe to talk.

So one day, we agreed to meet up at work on a Saturday. I was there first, so I waited until an hour went by. I called her. She had been crying.

"What's the matter?" I asked.

She said, "I stopped at the store to buy you a present, and I ran into Chrissy."

I answered, "So?"

"Ramsey, I can't do this anymore," she said and hung up the phone.

I tried to call her over and over again all weekend long. I waited for her to show up on Monday. I received a phone call about eleven o'clock. It was Liz's husband.

"I don't know what happened between you two, and I don't want to know, but officially, today, she resigns."

Fuck! What the hell caused all this? Did she finally get a conscience? Months later, I heard through a mutual friend that she had left her husband and kid and moved out of state. I never got closure with Liz. I will always wonder what caused her change of heart. I spent months crying, late at night. I couldn't hold it together anymore. I fell into a deep depression and started down that same comfortable road I had traveled before with drugs and alcohol. One night Chrissy came into the bedroom. She looked at me with the saddest look I'd ever seen on her.

"Ram, I need to know something," she said.

I looked up at her from the bed. I knew it wasn't going to be good.

"Are you having an affair?" she asked.

"No," I answered.

"Are you in love with someone else?" she asked, but this time with her voice quivering.

I studied her face, looking for some forgiveness in her eyes. I turned away from her, tears streaming down my face.

"Ramsey?"

"Yes, Chrissy, I am in love with someone else," I said, sobbing.

She calmly turned around and walked out of her room. She didn't say anything, but I heard her call her sister. The next day, Chrissy's sister and some friends showed up with a U-Haul trailer. I stayed in bed the entire time they moved Chrissy's belongings out of our house. Chrissy never said another word, and I didn't chase her out the door. Somewhere back in my mind, I think I still resented Chrissy for the abortion. Or at least not letting me be a part of it. But there wasn't a day that I didn't think about Liz.

# CHAPTER 9
# THE SADNESS

*The Lord is close to the broken hearted and saves those
who are crushed in spirit.*

*—Psalm 34:18*

It slipped up on me like an eclipse. The sadness that hits you in the pit of your stomach when you get the call that someone close to you has died. But it goes beyond that. It stretches into a vast darkness that completely surrounds your entire being. I could smell the staleness of what used to be fresh air. Everything I ate or drank tasted foul and caused my gag reflexes to work overtime. I puked every meal and lost the weight I had worked so hard to pack on. I faked my way through relationships with my siblings, my parents, my coworkers, and every other part of an otherwise decent life. No one suspected when I returned to my home alone that there was a whole different side of me slowly killing every living cell of life like a cancer.

I found ways to minimize the sadness until I could fall asleep. Besides the same old self-medication of alcohol and drugs that I found to be reliable, I looked for other ways. I once found myself in a drunken stupor, naked, crying on the bathroom floor. The razor blade in my trembling hand sliced into each of my upper thighs, carving her first initial: *L*. The blood oozed from the open wound, and the tears were so many that they fell into the wound, the salt finding every nerve ending, sending shocks of satisfactory pain—a punishment, but a temporary cure for the anguish. I would press the wounds with my palms and lift my hands into the air, part praying and part screaming at God, "Is this what You want from me?" I justified this act as some sort of an Old Testament way of a blood sacrifice. I knew God was watching me, and by including Him in this ritual, it couldn't be wrong. I had to be punished. On more than one occasion, I stood in front of the mirror and punched myself in the face, just trying to beat the feeling out of me. Why did Liz have to fuck up my life by leaving?

Only once during this period of sadness did I think about the end. I believe I had what experts call a psychotic episode. I sat my pistol on the table and sat down across from it as if it were my guest for dinner. I sat and stared at it for a long time. I felt God's presence, so I pretended He was sitting in the chair in front of my pistol. I was drinking out of a bottle of tequila. I motioned the bottle to the empty chair and said, "I know you're here, God. You might as well drink up."

I saw the pistol move clockwise a half a turn.

"I don't have the guts to do it myself, so I want you to pick up that pistol and put me out of my misery," I told Him. "Be the almighty, merciful God that You are!"

The pistol moved back and forth on the table as if shaking its head no.

"No? Aren't You the merciful God? Then show Your mercy and put me out of my misery!"

The pistol rose up from the table and flew toward me, the barrel slamming into my forehead.

"There you go!"

I was shaking in anticipation, I saw the hammer go back, and I heard a click. No bang, just a click. It was still pressed against my head. I remember screaming, "No! Please have mercy! Dear, God, have mercy! Take me now!"

The pistol fell to the table, and I started sobbing. I woke up the next day on the floor. I couldn't believe I actually had gotten this low. I picked up the pistol—it was still loaded—and ejected the bullet from the chamber. I looked at the bullet, and the primer had a dent in it. It was a misfire. I also had small cuts and dried blood on my forehead. That figures. I get to keep going.

I started going out and picking up bar flies that looked like Liz just to punish myself. One night I went out with this pretty crazy chick. We had just had sex, and she was lying on the bed, while I sat in the living room in another drunken stupor. I had just lit up my last cigarette, and I watched the pool of water gather around the bottom of my formerly frosted glass of tequila. I thought, *I should have used a coaster.* I rubbed the beginning of a late-night hangover out of my head. I looked at the grease on my fingers from my hair. *Damn I need a shower.* I stared at the phone, somehow expecting Liz to call me. It was almost five o'clock in the morning, so that probably wasn't going to happen.

I looked in the other room, and I saw the woman I had gone out with. She was sound asleep already. Shit, she didn't even care that I was awake. *Karen, Katherine? Damn,* I thought, *I'd better remember before she wakes up.*

It had been three years since Liz walked out on me. Every day, I waited for the telephone to ring and to hear her voice. I stared at the phone. I don't know what made me think that day would be the day she'd call me. I felt it happening again. I realized the psychosis had taken over. I looked at the bed again. Liz was lying in my bed.

I blinked and shook my head. I was pretty sure it wasn't her. Still, I got up and walked over to take a better look. I sat at the edge of the bed. She had her back to me. She had the same curly brunette hair and slender body as Liz. I turned her slightly to get a glimpse of her face.

"Well, hey, baby," she moaned as she rubbed her eyes.

Oh God, it wasn't Liz. Never in a hundred years would she call me baby.

"Go back to sleep. It's only five," I whispered.

She put her arms around me, kissed my lips, and whispered into my ear, "Let's do round three."

I could smell the tequila and stale cigarettes on her breath. She was smiling, and I thought for a brief second I could see myself with her for a long time.

"OK, but I'll be right back. I need to clean up."

I went into the bathroom and stared at myself in the mirror. That bastard looking at himself could never forgive himself for letting Liz walk away. I punched myself hard in the face. I winced as the swelling started under my right eye and sent signals of pain to my brain. I put the lid down on the toilet seat, took the towel off the rack, and began to sob into the towel.

*God, I miss her,* I thought. My friend, my lover. I was cheating on everyone who walked into my life as long as I held onto her. I looked at the scars below the tattoos on my arms where I had carved myself trying to remove the pain. I went to the sink, turned on the cold water, and washed the tears from my face and eyes. The swelling below my right eye was larger. I panicked as I thought of how I would explain it. I splashed cold water on it, but it would not go down.

I sank to my knees and began to pray, "Please, God, let her be gone when I get out of here, and let Liz be in her place." I crossed myself and stood up. I opened the medicine cabinet and pulled out a single-edged razor blade. I sat on the toilet seat again, and I cut a small cross on the inside of both of my thighs and watched the blood slowly pool along the cuts. "Liz, I do this for you," I chanted softly.

"Hey, what are you doing in there, baby?" Katie yelled.

*That's it! Katie. Goddamn it! Katie is her name. Whew.* "I'll be right out, Katie."

I cleaned up the cuts with alcohol and held back the screams of pain. I looked in the mirror and saw my swollen eye. I shook my head and wondered when it would stop. I flushed some cold water on my face and turned off the light and walked out.

"Well, it sure took you long enough. I almost gave up, baby," Katie said.

I walked over and stood by the bed. "Hey, Katie, please call me Ram."

"Aww, you don't like being called baby?" she said as she stroked my legs.

"Hey, I got a better idea. Why don't you just go," I said as I backed away from her.

"What the hell happened to you? You're bleeding!" she yelled as she got up on her knees in the bed. "How did you get those cuts?"

"I cut myself shaving" was the best answer I could muster.

She jumped off the bed and started gathering her clothes. "What kind of a freak are you? You need some fucking help. And, by the way, who the fuck is this Liz bitch you called me last night, you sick fuck?"

I coldly looked at her, gritted my teeth, and said, "Don't you ever mention her name again."

"Ram, don't worry, baby. I'm not coming back. Asshole!" And she slammed the door as she walked out.

I sat down and stared at the phone. *Please, Liz, I beg you, please call today. Please release me.*

# CHAPTER 10
# I NEED TO FIND PEACE

*And the peace of God, which surpasses all understanding,*
*will guard your hearts and minds in Christ Jesus.*

*—Philippians 4:7*

I had just walked in from the hospital, and I was thinking about finding a reason to go back. I had to get my stomach pumped and answer five thousand stupid fucking questions because I apparently tried to poison myself. This wouldn't have happened if I had just gone home a couple of nights ago.

I started a second job about three months before. I started working security at a music venue with Fred, a childhood buddy of mine. We were working the White Stripes concert, and the crowd was pretty funky, but we still had an easy go of it.

We lit out as soon as it was over and went to Fred's with a couple of young ladies who Fred had conned into believing we were Jack White's bodyguards and we would see him later that evening. Fred and the girls did a couple of bumps of cocaine at the table, while I unwound on three really deep bong hits of absolutely the best bud I had ever had. That Fred really knew how to party.

I took Lilli, the older of the two, into Fred's spare room where we drank the last half of tequila out of a bottle Fred had. We started making out, and before I could lose my buzz, I found myself underneath her naked body, while she straddled me. Jesus, she looked like an angel. It scared me because Lilli had an expression that was almost supernatural. She was fucking beautiful I tell you. And she actually glowed. In my stoned stupor, I was trying to figure out if she was a ghost the entire time she was bringing herself to climax. Damn, what a distraction. She rolled off me, and I got up on one elbow and looked at her.

"What?" she asked.

I shook my head. I asked, "What just happened?"

"You mean the fucking?" She looked puzzled.

"Forget it." I figured whatever it was must have been due to my altered state.

She laughed. "Man, you really need to get laid more often."

She was right. I already liked her. That was my big mistake. She had that curly dark hair, thin wispy body, and a smile just like Liz's. *Here we go again.* But it was something else.

"Jack White's not really coming, is he?" she asked.

"No, but we did work security."

She said, "I know. You went through my purse at the door. Thanks for letting me keep my little bottle."

I laughed. "No problem. You're hot, so it was an easy decision."

"So you would have taken it off an ugly fat girl?"

"Absofuckinglutely!" I joked back.

She smiled and pretended to slap my face. "Bad boy."

I rolled over and grabbed a cigarette off the nightstand. I turned to look at her. "Want one?" *That's it,* I thought. Her eyes. She had blue eyes that lit up when she talked.

"I'm trying to quit," she responded.

I started getting that feeling in my stomach again. I think I'm falling for this one. I stood up to put on my clothes. Lilli was watching me.

"What happened to your legs?" she asked, looking at the cross shapes I had cut into my legs last year, which were now scars.

"Cut myself shaving." I shrugged. I rushed to put my pants on.

"Wait," she said.

She walked over and got on her knees right in front of me. I wanted to scream at her to get the fuck away from me. She was looking into my eyes as she started undoing my pants again. She pulled them down, exposing the scars. I gritted my teeth and clinched my fists. My body was shaking as she touched each scar gently, stopping to kiss each one. I gently pushed her head away.

"Relax, Ramsey," she whispered. "It's OK. Shh, it's OK."

A tear rolled down my left cheek and fell onto her arm.

She looked up at me. "It's OK."

I pulled away from her, fell onto the bed, and began sobbing into the pillow. Oh, yeah, fucking loud, wailing sobs.

Fred knocked on the door. "Hey, you guys all right in there?"

Lilli said, "He's OK. It's just a bad dream."

"Fuck, dude!" Fred exclaimed as he walked away.

Lilli was still naked, and I could feel her breasts against me as she comforted me. I probably cried like that for a good five minutes. I was exhausted. Fucking Liz! I think, right then, I realized I really hated her for never allowing me closure. We fell asleep just like that, across the bed with Lilli pressed against me.

The next morning, I woke up and slid out from under Lilli. She stirred and got up with me. She told me she had a good time, but neither of us brought up the previous night. I figured any chance with her I'd lost by showing my pussy side with the waterworks. She opened her purse, got out a pen and paper, and wrote her number down. She pressed it into my hands and said to call her sometime. She tiptoed up and went to kiss me, and I turned my cheek to her.

She kissed my cheek, and I walked out. Fred wasn't awake, so I let myself out and drove home.

I got home that morning and started checking my messages. *Beep,* my mom. *Beep,* fucking sales call. *Beep,* "Hi, Ramsey. Sorry I haven't called. I'm in town and thought I would say hi. Call me at two-one-two-six-*beep*."

Fuck! I played the message again. It was, without a doubt, Liz. After five fucking years, she calls me, and all I get is a partial number. I pulled the machine off the table and smashed it on the floor. I panicked. I checked caller ID on the phone.

Mom.

Fucking 1-800 number.

Private number.

I immediately hit star sixty-nine, and the voice on the phone said it could not complete the call. I threw up right on the kitchen floor where I was standing. I went to my knees and kept getting sick. I can't believe she's here. I cleaned up the floor and sat at the table with my head in my hands, waiting for her to call back. I didn't move all morning. Not to drink, eat, piss, or anything. A depression had fallen over me, and I thought I was dying.

It was around seven o'clock that evening, and I went to the liquor cabinet and opened a bottle of tequila. I shot the bottle in one take. I thought I was going to puke again. My jaw tightened, and the back of my throat gagged while I waited for it to come up. Nothing. I went to the medicine cabinet, popped a mouthful of Vicodin, poured a double shot of tequila out of a new bottle, and came back to the table to wait for the phone. That's the last thing I remember before I woke up with tubes shoved down my throat in the hospital.

Fred drove me home. He asked if I wanted him to stay, but I really didn't want the company. I promised him I'd go to sleep and he need not worry. What a fucked-up evening last night was. I had just turned off the lights and was heading down the hall to my bedroom, where I was either going to crash or die, when I heard the doorbell.

*Liz!* My heart started beating wildly. She'd finally come home. I couldn't wait to kiss her and tell her how much I loved her. I went to the door, hyperventilating, with my mind buzzing. I pulled the door open with such force that it banged against the wall.

"Oh!" Lilli exclaimed.

Shit, it was Lilli, not Liz. She must have seen the disappointment on my face.

"Are you OK?" she asked.

I stood there for a moment, trying to gather my thoughts. "Sure, I'm fine," I said, standing there with the door wide open.

Lilli looked around me into the house, trying to peer around the corner. "Can I come in?"

"Look, I really don't feel like company tonight."

She started, "Oh. The way you opened the door, I thought you might be expecting someone."

"Sure, why not. Come in," I answered.

She walked in, and I shut the door behind her.

"Fred told me what happened, and I wanted to see you," Lilli said.

"Fred has a big fucking mouth," I said with gritted teeth.

"Do you want me to leave?"

"No. Sorry, it's just been a weird couple of days."

The phone rang once. I looked at it. A second ring, and I walked over toward the phone. A third ring, and Lilli walked over and stood in front of the phone: "Leave it." A fourth ring, and I grabbed her by the shoulders to move her. She reached up and kissed me. A fifth ring, and I was still kissing Lilli.

It was now or never. I had to stop. I reached around Lilli, picked up the phone, and put it back on the receiver. I've never regretted not answering the phone. Lilli and I stayed together for a year before she moved back to Michigan to take a great job. We talked on the phone sometimes, but we never saw each other again. She was an awesome woman. She was loving, nurturing, and damned sexy. She taught me how to have peace.

# CHAPTER 11

# TIME FOR SOME FUN

*A time to weep, a time to laugh, a time to mourn, and a
time to dance.*

*—Ecclesiastes 3:4*

I started doing some freelance work. One of the first clients I
picked up was a construction company. It was a family-owned
business out of Southwest Arkansas near the Texas border. They
primarily served the Ark-La-Tex region, but the youngest son,
Keith, had married a girl from Austin, so he opened up shop and
became successful overnight. That guy was one of the sharpest
business minds I ever met. He could turn a turd into gold. He was
a tall, blond-haired, blue-eyed sculpted rock of a man. He wore
tailored shirts, drove a fully loaded Escalade, and made it a point
to tell everyone how much money he made. He was about five years
younger than me, and we had a great working relationship.

But Keith was a piece of work. He was the biggest racist I had
ever met. This was the early '90s, and the only time I heard the *N*

word was around a few select old people and rednecks. But this didn't fit. He was a professional and pretty well off. He also treated women as badly as he did blacks. One day, I hired a contractor whom I used occasionally to go to Keith's office and pick something up for me. She called me crying and told me that she would never go there again. He had twice, in the thirty minutes she was there, made sexual advances toward her so obvious that she felt threatened. I called him on it, and all he could say was, "I can't believe you haven't fucked her." No apology, just that line.

One day he called me and told me to stop by his office. I took off at lunch from my regular job and went by to see what he needed.

"Let's go talk this over at lunch," he said.

I figured we would be about an hour, so I jumped in his Escalade, and we chatted about business while we were on the road. We pulled right up to the valet parking of a local strip club. I had only been a couple of times to a strip club, back when I was young and had no money, so it wasn't my thing.

We had a nice steak and lobster lunch, and Keith would chase the girls away when they came up to us while we were eating. It was obvious he was a regular as he asked about one of the girls by name. We wrapped up lunch with a couple of shots of tequila.

He toasted as we were about to slam it down: "Here's to pretty women and big titties."

I slammed mine down. Oh, my old familiar friend, tequila. About that time, a cute black girl walked up to our table. She came and sat on my lap. I looked at Keith, and he was doing a slow burn.

He told her, "Talk to your manager. You're not supposed to be at this table."

I was stunned. What the hell was that supposed to mean?

Keith waved the manager to our table. Keith looked at him and said in a low, but cold voice, "I've told you before, if you want me to keep coming here and spending my money, I don't want any goddamned niggers at our table."

I was in total shock.

Danny, the manager, said, "She's new, Keith. I didn't know you were coming in, so I forgot to tell her."

Keith gave the manager a twenty-dollar bill and said, "Try and remember next time."

I was looking at Keith in disbelief. I had only heard stories of this kind of shit from my daddy when he talked about growing up in East Texas. But this was the '90s, and she was hot!

I was just about to tell Keith I was ready to leave, when that song from *From Dusk Till Dawn* came on. You know the one—"After Dark," where Salma Hayek dances to it right before she turns into a freaking vampire. I looked onstage to see who the hell had the nerve to play that song, much less dance to it. And there she was, this young brunette with thick thighs like a figure skater and very large breasts. She was dancing to the song in such a sexy rhythm that I was spellbound. Man, what a pro. I walked up to the stage to tip her, and I couldn't take my eyes off hers.

She had beautiful blue eyes, light blue. Yes, I'm that guy who looks into a half-naked woman's eyes. She held my gaze as she got closer to me. She grabbed my shirt collar with both hands and pulled my head into her crotch. Me being so tall, that's where my head wound up. Then she pushed me away, bent down, and asked me my name. Fuck, after that, I couldn't remember where I was, much less my name. I told her, and she kissed my neck, my clue to tip her. I tipped her well and asked her to come to my table. I knew I was locked in now. I wasn't going back to work.

I was nervous as a high-school boy on a first date while I waited for her. Keith had found some play thing and was no longer paying attention to me. Not a real big loss, the prick. Anyway, after about fifteen minutes, she came walking over to my table.

"Buy you a shot of tequila?" I asked.

"I'm not old enough, silly. I'm only twenty," she said, holding up her arm that had an underage band on her wrist.

The band was what they put on people who are under twenty-one so no one will buy or sell them an alcoholic drink. Here I was, thirty-five years old, almost twice her age, but I couldn't convince myself to send her on her way. Two things I didn't necessarily find attractive, young women and big boobs, and here she was, both in the flesh.

So moving ahead I said, "I'm Ramsey."

"I'm Natasha," she responded.

"Is that your stage name or real name?" I asked, guessing it was her stage name.

"Nope, it's my real name. My mom is Russian."

"*Pree-vee-et,*" I sounded out, which was hello in Russian.

She said something else in Russian that I didn't understand, and we laughed. So we continued with the small talk, and I bought her a Red Bull, and we figured it was time to put her to work. She started a lap dance for me. She slowly danced (it was a great slow song), and she wiggled on my lap, pressing her breasts into my face. She then straddled me and put her mouth right up to mine without touching it, and we breathed kisses and fake kissed each other, heating each other up. She moved over to my most vulnerable weak spot on my body, my neck, and began kissing and sucking it so lightly, bringing my excitement level to unbearable. The song ended just in time. She stayed on my lap, straddling me, as we talked about where we were from, our significant-other status, and a couple of interesting tidbits about each other.

Keith and I stayed the rest of the night until the shift change, about eight o'clock. I had no idea how much I'd spent on Natasha and didn't really care. She gave me her phone number and asked me to call her the next day. I didn't. I also figured she did that with all the guys, so why bother? She wasn't working the next day, so I went in the day after, just to see her again. As soon as I walked in, she came over from the bar and asked why I hadn't called her. Great, as if I needed this shit from a stripper. I explained that I thought she was bullshitting me, so I didn't bother. She asked if I was staying late. I told her I had a dinner date, so I couldn't. She asked me to pick her up after her shift was over at two o'clock in the morning. I figured why not. I'd give her a chance. So I went on my date, and we had a great time. My date was a setup from one of my workmates. She was a nice lady, but a bit overweight and seemed to have some issues with her ex-husband. We made out a bit, but I lied and said I had to go out of town on business the next day, so I left her early. Truth be told, she wasn't what I liked in a woman. I was a skinny-girl, B-cup kind of guy. The curiosity had gotten the best of me with Natasha. There she was as I rolled up in my SUV, my little titty dancer waiting on me.

She got in and kissed me hello. I found it kind of awkward. I don't know why, but I think I'm a bit of a slow mover sometimes. The thing is, this girl was half my age, and I couldn't imagine there being anything more than physical attraction keeping us together. We went to my place, where I rolled a joint while we talked about why she was dancing—of course, to pay her way through school. And out of the blue, she just said, "What I really want is to find someone to take care of me."

Ya think?

"I'll live with you, fuck you, and do whatever else you want, but I just want to be taken care of. I need it!" she said.

"Slow down, sister," I replied. "I'm doing OK by myself here. I don't answer to anyone and can do anything I want, anytime."

She came up to me where I was sitting on the couch and said, "Look, try it for a little while. If it doesn't work for you, I'll go."

I didn't believe it for a second. But looking into those eyes as she unbuttoned her shirt and watching her tilt her head to undo her bra as her massive, natural breasts spilled out was probably what did it.

"OK, but really, do you have a place to go if this doesn't work?" I asked.

"Don't worry. It will work."

We cemented our deal with a really long session of crazy love-making. For being twenty, she was quite experienced. As with all men with hard dicks, any caution I had was gone.

The next morning, when I woke, she was already gone. *Good,* I thought. *She doesn't have a key.* I walked out to get my morning paper, and I was shocked to see my brand-new Chevy Tahoe gone. I could only muster one loud yelled word, "Fuck!" I ran inside and looked at my dresser where my wallet and keys were supposed to be. Oh, hell yes, they were gone. I didn't waste any time. I called the cops and told them that I had been robbed. Of course the detective they sent out to investigate was a female. So as God's sense of humor would have it, I had to suffer the consequences of telling her the story about how I hooked up with a twenty-year-old stripper, took her home, told her she could move in with me, had sex with her, and then had all my shit stolen the next day. Oh, yeah, I can't even begin to recall all the sarcastic, snide remarks Austin's finest had to lay on me. It was painful to admit to being a complete dumbass. They tracked my Tahoe down on the other side of San Antonio, wrecked, of course. I was able to cancel my credit cards before too much got out of hand. And, of course, Keith had a laugh at my expense and would bring it up almost every time we got together. Even after this stupid ordeal, I was finally beginning to get out of my funk.

You see, they say money can't buy happiness, but I'm living proof: if you spend enough on tequila and a well-trained stripper, you can put a Band-Aid on your entire fucked-up situation. They will tell you they love you, they will fuck you, and they will rob you blind. It doesn't matter. I started losing myself in my work during the day so I could pay for my night. The more money I made, the more I paid for those few hours of sunshine in my sad, dark, and lonely world. So my new journey began.

I took a night job with the strip club as an assistant manager and bouncer. They just wanted a big guy in the room to keep the shit from getting out of hand. It paid pretty well for a part-time gig. Some of the regular customers would tip me real good to look the other way so they could get a hand job or even a blow job. I didn't give anybody any shit and usually didn't get any back. I just drank tequila, smoked cigarettes, and walked the floor.

This job gave me the opportunity to meet some pretty nice ladies and some fucked-up ones as well. I stayed away from the trash, and I made it clear which ones needed to stay out of my way. One night I met this cute little waitress who had just started that week. She didn't dance but waited on tables. She made pretty good money because she knew how to work the customers. Her name was Kiki. Her real name was Kathryn, but everyone she liked called her Kiki. What a girl. She was twenty-six, had short auburn hair, stood five foot five, and weighed maybe 130 pounds right out of the shower. I got a kick every time I heard that East Tennessee accent roll off her tongue. I think, at the time we met, I was twenty years older than her, but we discovered during our chats when things got slow that we had a lot in common. She was also a pothead, and she had a boyfriend who treated her like shit. One night, right before closing time, she asked me if she could catch a ride. Me being the Good Samaritan type, I said sure. She didn't live far, so I got the valet to bring my Tahoe around. She jumped in the passenger seat, looked over at me, and grinned. I grinned back and started out of the parking lot, and before I could get into the intersection, she yelled, "Stop!" I was startled as I thought she had forgotten something. Instead, she jumped over, almost in my lap, and started kissing me like she was never going to see me again. I had to push her away to get a breath.

"Whoa! Are you OK?" I asked.

She said, "Let's drive around a bit, OK?"

I figured I was out anyway, so why not. I pulled out of the parking lot onto the main drag. We hadn't gone a mile to the first traffic light. She made that move again. We kissed deep, wet, open-mouthed kisses. God, she drove me crazy. A horn honked, and we kept kissing. It honked again, and I started driving, trying to see out of my left eye while still kissing Kiki. She pulled away and laughed. I looked over at her, grinning. I could see that she was high. It was funny to see her that way.

"Kiki, where are we going?" I asked.

She said, "Do we have to go anywhere? Let's just hang out."

This was a different Kiki tonight. We never talked about any kind of attraction to each other, and even though I thought she was hot, I never made a move. I pulled into a parking lot of a professional building that was under construction.

"Talk to me, Kiki," I said as I looked into her eyes.

She started, "My boyfriend threw me out, and I need a place to crash."

Fuck! Just my luck. I'd already had one dose of stupidity, and after all of that kissing, I really wanted her. She pulled out a joint, lit it up, and passed it to me. It was quiet for a while. I took a hit and assessed my situation.

"Hang on, baby. I'll make a call."

She jumped over onto my lap, straddling and facing me. I dropped the still-lit joint onto the floorboard, and as we began kissing again, I could smell the skunk smell of pot coming from the floorboard. She pulled off her top, exposing her breasts. I couldn't resist her and began kissing her all over her upper body.

We fell into a deep passionate moment that I can't begin to describe, but I will always remember. I hurriedly unzipped my pants, she lifted her skirt, and we started having sex in the front seat of my SUV. I saw lights out of the corner of my eye but was so caught up in what we were doing that I didn't notice the patrol car that had pulled up next to us. *Tap, tap, tap* was the sound on the window. A flashlight shone in the window. Kiki freaked, grabbed her top, and was trying to dive onto the floorboard, while I was trying to get my pants up.

"Sir, when you get situated, please step out of the car," the officer said.

Fuck, I couldn't believe it. I wanted to finish with Kiki first, but my judgment had not been impaired that much. I pulled up my pants and stepped out, zipping my zipper. I looked back to see Kiki covering her face. I could hear her, but what I thought was crying was uncontrollable laughter. I looked at the officer, embarrassed but grinning.

"Ram, what the fuck are you doing?" I couldn't believe my eyes. The cop was a high-school friend of mine.

"Geez, Griff, you kinda caught me at a bad time."

He grinned and pulled me to the back of the car. "How much pot is in the car?" he asked.

"I swear, Griff, just the one joint that is on the floorboard." I wasn't really sure how much Kiki had on her, so that was the truth.

I was relieved that it was Griff because as embarrassed as I was to face him, anyone else, and it would have been much worse.

"Look, I don't know if you're finished or not, but I suggest you get a room, Ram. Damn, you act like such a fucking kid. Get going, and be sure to tell your brother hello for me," he said and got back into his car.

I walked over to the car, and Kiki was still laughing.

"Who was that guy?" she asked.

I explained the benefits of living in the town I grew up in and what I had on my old buddy Griff. When we were in high school, he had robbed a gas station, and I was the driver. He didn't get much, and the dumbass had used his hand in his jacket as a gun. A couple of months later, at that same gas station, the owner shot and killed a guy pulling that same shit. We never talked about it. Ever!

As she started to move toward me again, I stepped out of the car, called a buddy of mine, and asked if we could crash there for the night. I wasn't going to take her to my place. I just wasn't ready for that. He said it would be fine, but only one night.

"Well, I got us a place for the night," I told Kiki.

She laughed. "I'm so fucking horny. I hope it's not far."

Needless to say, I got there as fast as I could. Kiki and I wound up hanging together for about eight months. She wanted to move in, but I just wasn't ready for that commitment. Her mom got sick, so she suddenly moved back to Tennessee. We kept in touch for a couple of months. That girl was fun. I sure missed her but moved on quickly.

# CHAPTER 12

# DEATH IS ALL AROUND ME

*And I looked, and behold, a pale horse! And its rider's name was Death, and Hades followed him. And they were given over a fourth of the earth, to kill with sword and with famine and pestilence and by wild beasts of the earth.*

*—Revelation 6:8*

After Kiki left, I started running around with Keith again. He had gone back to Arkansas for a few months to be with his dying father and was now back. But every couple of weeks, he would go back and tend to the business there. One day he called me up.

"Ram, I fucked up. Trish wants a fucking divorce, and she is taking my kids away."

Trying to get him to open up was difficult. He was as shallow as they come. But this time he spilled his guts. It turned out she caught him fucking one of the strippers from a club in Dallas. He always had that going on the side but had never gotten caught. I guess, with all the other shit he did, it was bound to happen.

"Come up and hang out with me for the weekend. I need some company."

So he made the flight arrangements, called me back, and told me he'd pick me up at Dallas Fort Worth the next day. We would drive the rest of the way to his family farm between Dallas and the Arkansas border.

I flew out with just a bag of overnight clothes, and he picked me up around two o'clock that afternoon. It was July, and already the temperatures had reached one hundred degrees several times that month. It was just another sweltering Texas July afternoon. He pulled his Escalade right up to the passenger-pickup area right on time. I jumped in and quickly enjoyed the air conditioning. He looked like he was already high and like he hadn't slept in a couple of days. He had his pearl-handled 9-mm pistol and a box of ammo on the seat between us. I didn't think much of it as I figured we might let off some steam when we got to his place by shooting a few rounds.

"I got some tequila, some blow, some weed, and this beautiful motherfucker right here," he said as he picked the pistol up off the seat.

I didn't really pay much attention to it, but looking back, I should have seen it as trouble. We began the long familiar trip on I-30 toward the farm. As we got about forty-five miles east of Dallas, the right front tire blew out. Keith immediately dialed his roadside service on his cell phone. It continuously gave him an all-circuits-busy signal. He waited for fifteen minutes, called again, and got the same results.

"Goddamn it!" he shouted as he threw the phone into the truck. "I can't get a fucking signal. Try your phone."

Same shitty signal with my phone, too. We sat in the air-conditioned truck with a damned flat tire as cars continually passed us. Not one person stopped to offer assistance.

"I guess I'll change the son of a bitch myself!" he screamed as he got out and slammed the truck door.

I laughed quietly to myself; Keith wasn't used to manual labor. He had everything done for him—his oil changes, his car washes, his lawn service, and his laundry. Then I thought, *Hell, I'm not either.* I got out to help him anyway.

After forty-five minutes and a hell of lot of sweat and cusswords in the hot Texas sun, we managed to get the tire changed, and he picked up and angrily tossed the other tire in the back. He said he would take it into town in the morning and have it fixed. We were soaking wet and miserable. Keith was madder than I had ever seen him. You could just see on his face he was holding in an explosion. We got in the Escalade and started back on the road. We had gone another forty miles when the air conditioner quit blowing cool air.

"Now what?" he asked. He angrily jerked the truck over and slammed to a stop. We got out, and he popped open the hood. He looked around under the hood. Crazy bastard had no idea what he was looking at, so he slammed it back down and screamed, "Fuck!" He gave the hood a good pounding with his fist and said, "I don't give a shit. We're gonna keep going, and I'll have someone come out tomorrow." We got back in, and he sat there for a minute. Neither one of us said anything. Finally, he said, "Fuck it," as he reached under the seat and pulled out a vial of coke. He pulled a CD out of the visor where he kept them.

"Ha! Billie fucking Holliday." He laughed. He poured a couple of big lines of coke and snorted it off the CD. "Here, you want a bump?" he said as he motioned the vial my way.

I had been clean from that shit for a while, so I declined.

"Goddamn! You've gone pussy on me."

I didn't want him pissed any more than he already was, so I reached around and got the tequila from the backseat. I cracked the seal, drank a third of the bottle, and handed it to him.

"Now you're talking, you crazy bastard!" he said.

We rolled the windows down, he turned the music up, and we began our trip again. Only this time, he was driving pretty damned fast. I figured we were going to get pulled over, but it didn't happen. What started off as a relaxing trip now had Keith crazy. The flat, the air conditioner, and the hot Texas sun beating down on us just added to the already stressful situation of his marriage falling apart. A few minutes later, we turned onto the county road that would take us to his farm. Man, was I glad to get closer to getting off the highway with him?

We were about ten miles from the farm when we came upon a car pulled to the side of the road with an old black woman standing outside of it. She had a white handkerchief and was dabbing the sweat from her chest. The car had a flat tire. He quickly pulled over and almost jumped outside. I sat in the passenger seat and wondered what the hell he was doing.

"You need some help, ma'am?" he asked.

"Yessa, I guess I do," she responded. "I got one of those flat tires, and I don't know how to fix it. And it's plum too hot to be standing out here in the sun."

Well, we had already changed one tire today, so another one wasn't going to hurt us any worse. I guess Keith had calmed down enough because he looked at me and said, "Come on, Ram. Let's help the lady out." He asked the lady her name.

"Estherlene Q. Washington, and I'm eighty-nine years old. I was going to visit my daughter in Greenville."

Keith said, "Glad to meet you, Mrs. Washington. You can just call me Mr. Johnson, and this here is Mr. Jackson, and we're just passing through."

I looked over at Keith, and he winked and smiled at me. I couldn't read him, but I was suspicious given what I already knew about him being a racist. We began to change the tire, while the old woman rambled on and on some old bullshit about how her family had settled here when the slaves were freed and most of the young kids moved away. I couldn't wait to get this good deed done, especially with Keith being so unstable. When we finished, I put the flat tire in the trunk.

Keith said, "Well, Mrs. Washington, you're ready to go. You need to get that tire fixed when you get to your daughter's house."

I was knelt down on the passenger side of Keith's Escalade, wiping my hands in the grass to clean off the grease and dirt. I heard Keith say, "Wait just a second before you go. I have something for you." He walked back to the truck just as I was standing up. He grabbed his wallet off the dash, picked the pistol up off the seat, and put it in his beltline behind his back.

"Keith," I said.

He looked over and said, "Hey, I'm just going to give her a twenty to help get the tire fixed."

I said it again, this time a little louder. "Keith!"

He had a blank look on his face.

I watched him pull a bill out of his wallet, so I calmed down. I opened the door of the Escalade and was leaning against it with my foot on the side runner. I looked up ahead at Mrs. Washington, who was now sitting in the car waiting for Keith to return.

Keith bent over her window and handed her the twenty. "This should help you get the tire fixed when you get back," he said.

She looked up at him and smiled. "My goodness, Mr. Johnson, you don't have to do that." She chuckled.

I watched in horror and disbelief at what happened next.

Keith said, "I want you to have this, too." He stood up and quickly reached around, while she still had the twenty in her hands and was looking it over. He wheeled the pistol around and fired the first round directly into her forehead. I watched as pieces of her skull, brain matter, and blood spattered out of the back of her head. He fired a second shot as she was going backward in the car. I saw her jerk again. He fired again. I couldn't move.

Keith yelled, "Goddamn, that felt good! Wooeee!"

I was frozen.

"Come on, let's go." In a flash Keith was already back at the truck.

I was in shock as I jumped into the truck. He started it, and we headed up the road. He slammed on the brakes.

"Fuck, we have to go back!"

I wasn't even listening. I was still shaking and trying to process the whole scene again. He put it in reverse, slammed on the brakes, and calmly walked back to the car. I turned to watch him as he calmly took out his handkerchief and studied it for a moment. It was as though he was unaware of what he just did. He took the handkerchief and neatly began to wipe down the places we had touched on the newly changed tire. He wiped each lug nut with care. He walked around the car and looked around for the three spent shells. He decided it was time to hurry. He found two near the car on the road. He looked for the third but could not find it. "Get out and help me find the last shell, you motherfucker!" he yelled to me. I never moved.

He got back in the Escalade and threw his gun in the seat. I looked at the gun. I should have picked it up and shot him. He spun out as we left the scene. He was driving like a man possessed. I looked over, and at times we topped ninety per hour down the county road trying to hurry to the farm.

"You'd better snap out of it. You're a part of this, too!" he yelled.

"Are you a fucking psycho? What the fuck did you kill her for, you asshole?" I screamed back. I was starting to come to life. "Let me out of this fucking truck!" I screamed again.

As quick as a flash, he picked up the pistol and pressed it against my forehead. "Your prints are on the tire, the jack, and the lug wrench in the trunk. You're fucked. You might as well have pulled the trigger," he calmly told me.

I was fucked. I'd done some horrible shit and been in stupid positions but nothing as hopeless as where I was at that time in my life.

I was truly fucked. I did do it. Everything at the scene had my prints on it except the twenty-dollar bill and the missing spent shell. "What about the twenty and the shell?" I asked him. "Seems like you're just as fucked."

Just as I said that, up ahead a cop car was heading toward us, slowing down with his lights on. Just as we were upon him, the officer hit the siren. *Woop-woop.* The officer stuck out his arm to wave us over. What I didn't know until later was that the deputy was just making a routine traffic stop.

We kept going, and Keith really put the foot to the floor as we passed him. I turned and watched the deputy make a U-turn and follow us.

"Just pull over, you sick fuck!" I screamed as I reached for the steering wheel.

Keith still had the pistol in his hand, and he hit me hard right above my left eye with the muzzle. Immediately, blood started flowing, and I was woozy. He had really cracked me good.

"There was nobody around for miles. How would the cop know what the hell happened back there? There's no way anyone found her yet."

I was out of it again, and as far as I was concerned, Keith was trying to reconcile the situation with himself. I looked around, and the deputy was gaining on us. Keith saw it, too, so he slammed on his brakes. As he did, the deputy's car rammed the Escalade's rear, and in an explosion of noise, glass, and metal, both vehicles went into the ditches on opposite sides of the road from each other.

I was pinned in on my side, and between the blood in my face and the pain from being tossed around in the collision, I just leaned over in my seat. Keith reached for his pistol and immediately jumped out of the truck. I popped my head up to see what he was going to do. The deputy was struggling to get out of his car when Keith fired the first round into the windshield, barely missing the deputy's head.

The deputy quickly kicked out the passenger door and hid behind his car. He screamed toward Keith, "Drop your gun!"

"Fuck you, nigger!" screamed Keith, hiding behind his truck. It figured Keith would go there that soon because he was that big of a fucking racist.

"Why did you shoot at me?" asked the deputy.

"It doesn't matter anymore. That's why," Keith shouted as he fired another round into the deputy's car.

The deputy reached the radio and screamed into the microphone, "Officer needs assistance. Shots fired!"

I could hear the answer: "What's that, Washington?"

The deputy screamed, "Goddamn it! I said I need help!"

"What the hell do you mean, shots fired?" Keith fired another shot at the car, this time closer to the deputy's head.

"I'm on county road three-ten, just past the old place with the barn that is collapsed."

"You mean the Henry place?"

"I don't know. Just drive down three-ten toward I-Thirty until you find me. You can't miss me."

"We're on our way, Washington."

The deputy was dug in behind his car, and I heard him yell, "Why are you shooting at me?"

Keith was still drawn on him and screamed back, "The old lady, and you know it!"

"What old lady?"

I realized at that point that the deputy was just pulling us over for speeding. Keith fired two more rounds, and as the deputy ducked down, Keith reached in and grabbed the box of bullets from the seat. I had unbuckled my seat belt and was positioned to get out of the driver's side if I needed to. Keith looked at me and pointed the gun in my direction, motioning me to stay there. Then he released the magazine and started to reload. I turned my legs toward him and kicked him full in the chest with both feet, and he reeled backward.

He screamed, "I'm going to kill you, Ramsey!" He stood up and as he did, the deputy raised and fired his weapon and shot Keith in the leg, sending him tumbling back onto the ground. "Goddamn it, you black bastard. I'll kill you for that."

He lay on the ground, trying to reload. He got a couple of bullets into the clip and reloaded the gun. He was lying on his back on the ground looking at me, and he pointed, aimed, and fired, and I heard the bullet whiz right past me into the metal frame of the door behind me. The concussion of him firing the gun had me woozy again, and my ears were ringing.

The deputy screamed, "Drop the gun, or I'll shoot you again!"

This time, Keith wheeled around, got up on one knee, and shot at the deputy again. The slide of his pistol was back, and I saw the ejection port was open, but the deputy had already fired his weapon, hitting Keith in the torso twice. I watched him fall back. He was still moving, and his head was turned toward me, blood oozing out of his mouth as the deputy walked toward the truck.

The deputy was pointing the gun at me now and screamed, "Show me your hands!"

I had already had my hands up, but this time I shoved them out in front of me.

I looked over at Keith, and I realized he was dead. I'm not sure how I knew, but it didn't look like him. The deputy negotiated me out of the truck, and I was on the ground with my hands behind my back, in handcuffs, and still bleeding from the cut on my head. The other deputies began to arrive on the scene. I heard them talking, trying to sort out what had happened. I was lying still, feeling like I was going to pass out, but the adrenaline was still keeping me aware enough to comply with what they told me. The county sheriff arrived on the scene and walked up to where Deputy Washington was standing with the other deputies over by where Keith was lying on the ground.

He told Washington, "You need to come with me. I'm afraid I've got a bit of bad news."

He told the sheriff, "Look, Sheriff, I really need to finish this up. What is it, sir?"

"Your grandmother..."

I couldn't believe my fucking ears. The deputy let out a blood-curdling scream, ran over to where I was lying on the ground, and stomped my fucking head. I was already out. I didn't blame him.

I woke up in a hospital. I had no idea what day it was or even where I was. I had bandages around my torso and tubes in my veins. Between the pistol whipping and the head stomp, my head and part of my face was in bandages. I felt like I was dead. The only good news was the morphine I had running through my veins. There was a deputy in my room watching me. I found out I had a cracked skull and two broken ribs. Apparently, although it was denied, I got kicked in the ribs a couple of times as well. I spent another four days in the hospital in Greenville, Texas. I was interviewed over and over for three full days in the hospital. Between my lab reports coming back clean, my answers, and the evidence they had, I was released with no charges against me. Once again, the prayers of my grandmother and mother had kept me out of jail, or worse yet, prison. I didn't go to Keith's funeral. I heard a fight broke out among his family. What an appropriate send-off for that piece of shit. While I've been haunted by what I witnessed that day, I never missed him.

When I got back to work, I could hear the whispers. I knew what those gutless fucks thought about me. We negotiated a small severance package, and I was out a week later. Looking back, I probably didn't give them my best since it seemed like I was always fucked up. I still had some freelance clients, but nothing as big as Keith's account. My dad had been sick, and I wasn't the son I needed to be, so I went and helped Mom out as much as I could until Dad died. Mom kind of fell apart and died soon after. I don't know why I didn't focus on them as much as I should have. I was so busy fucking up my life that I never considered theirs. I started patching things up with my siblings after my dad's funeral. They forgave me but never understood why I fucked up my life the way I did. I got cleaned up again and stopped drinking and drugging. I started exercising, but I picked up cigarette smoking again. Without any of the other stuff, it was the only thing that would help me cope. I began getting to know my neighbors and was on my way to being a solid citizen. Nothing could change that.

A few months earlier, there were some new neighbors who moved in down the street that ended in front of my house. They were a Mexican couple, Ernesto and Isabella, with a couple of young kids. I usually saw her walking with her two small children in the evenings. Ernesto never walked with them. I never wondered why. The only time I saw him was when he was either leaning over the hood of or driving his 1951 Ford pickup. Man, what a beauty. It was painted cherry red, had glass packs and dual exhausts, and was riding low. I envied that guy, even if it was a lowrider.

One night, after I got out of the hospital, I was sitting in the carport, watching the sunset and smoking a cigarette. I heard screams coming from down the street. The kids ran out of Isabella and Ernesto's house, and right behind them ran a crying Isabella. She gathered her two kids up in her arms and started walking up the street toward my house. I tried to sit as low in my chair as I could as I didn't want any part of someone else's family shit. As soon as she got even with me, she looked up. I could see she had been hit pretty hard in the face as her eye was already starting to swell. She looked down and kept walking. I wanted to say something. I really did, but I could only watch as she kept walking.

Ernesto came running out of the house, slamming the door behind him. "Isabella! Isabella, I'm sorry. Come back in the house." He was running at a pretty fast gait and caught up with her quickly. He grabbed her arm and spun her around, almost making her drop the littlest child she was still carrying.

I got up out of my chair and threw my cigarette butt in the trash. As I did, I could see he had her by the arm pretty hard, and she wasn't resisting. He was whispering something to her as he dragged her back toward her house. I just watched them walk back. Isabella looked up at me, and I will never forget that look. She pleaded with her eyes for me to help her. I couldn't do it.

A few days later, I was going to work, and I saw Isabella with her two kids at the bus stop near the house. It wasn't that unusual since they only had one vehicle, that '51 Ford. And, of course, Ernesto drove it. But what was unusual was that Isabella had a suitcase with her. As I slowed down, I could see the purple around her eye where that bastard hit her. I waved, and she waved back. I figured she'd had enough of Ernesto and was heading back to Eagle Pass, where she was from.

I was sitting outside when Ernesto came home. It wasn't five minutes, and he was making a beeline to me.

"Hey, my wife and kids walk this way?"

Now that was my chance to help Isabella, so I said, "I haven't seen her all day."

He went back to his house, got in that old Ford, and burned rubber all to hell backing out of that driveway.

I kind of chuckled to myself. "She left your sorry ass."

About two weeks later, I saw Ernesto driving up the street, and I'd be damned if Isabella and the kids weren't sitting right in there with him. I figured I had it all wrong. Isabella must have taken a little trip instead of leaving him. They were just the coziest family all crammed in that truck. They seemed pretty happy and normal to me. Later that evening, Isabella and the kids walked by the house. She smiled and waved. I walked down to the curb to say hi.

"You back from vacation?" I asked.

She looked back toward her house. Ernesto was inside I guess.

"I left him," she said.

"I thought you might have," I replied.

"I called him Friday from my parents' house in Eagle Pass. He started crying and begged me to come back. I didn't know what else to do." She shook her head and looked back at her house.

I didn't know what to tell her. "I'm sure it's all right. You have the kids to think about."

Ernesto came outside, "Isabella!"

She turned to look at him, and then at me. She was scared, I could tell.

"Goodnight," she said and started walking back to her house.

It was real quiet around there for a couple of weeks.

One night, I was watching the news, and I heard screams outside. So I went to the door to see what the hell was going on.

"You whore!" Ernesto screamed at Isabella who was walking out the door. "I know you're fucking everyone in this whole neighborhood."

I went back inside. I had enough of this asshole, so I dialed 911.

I was waiting for a response when I heard a bang, followed by a second bang. I froze. My heart sank as I already knew what happened. The operator answered, and I hung up and walked outside. I could see Isabella in a heap down by the curb. Blood was coming out of her head, and it was a god-awful mess. Ernesto lay about fifteen feet from her and was still twitching. He still had the gun in his hand, and the side of his head was bloody; the damage was too hard to describe. I was sick to my stomach as I watched the two kiddos walk out of the house to find their mother. I yelled at another neighbor to take the kids back inside. The cops pulled up and took over the scene. That was the last time I saw Isabella. The funeral was in Eagle Pass, so I didn't go to it. After that, I sold my house and moved into an apartment. What I made on the sale I could live really good on for a while.

Then there was Alexis. I guess it was the second time she threw up that I fell in love with her. That poor wretched girl, so weak, helpless, and sick, needed me. It was because she needed me that my love was set in motion for her.

I had been working part time again at the strip club Keith and I used to go to for about six weeks after I sold my place. Alex, short for Alexis, was a waitress in the club. She was all of twenty-four years old, had cropped-short blond hair, and was skinny. She had that living-dead-girl look and could have passed for Edie Sedgewick's double. Her nose even wrinkled like hers when she smiled. For her age she was pretty responsible, never missing a day of work and always calling in if she was going to be late. She was quiet and kept to herself, offering up just a small amount of chitchat.

A day I won't forget—Carl, the club owner, asked me to check up on her on my way to work since Alex never showed up and didn't call. I drove to the address Carl gave me and found her unit, 131. It was a cheap apartment in the part of town that had recently seen a bit of decline. The roof was in dire need of repair as I noticed shingles missing in several places as I drove up to the unit. There were screens missing in several windows, and there was an overweight black woman leaning out of one of the apartment windows watching me walk up to the door.

I saw Alex's white Honda outside, and I figured she must be home. I knocked on the door. I looked up, and the black lady was still watching me. No answer, so I knocked again. No answer. This time I peered through the small window in the door and saw Alex lying on the floor near the couch.

"Alex," I yelled as I pounded on the door.

I looked through the window again and noticed she didn't stir. I tried the door handle, but it was locked. Go figure, locking the door in this neighborhood. I looked through the window again. Alex still hadn't moved.

I looked around for the office, went in, and found a meek, mouse-faced Indian man behind the desk. I told him that Alex was sick and that I was her father and came by to check up on her. He asked to see my ID. I told him I was actually Alex's stepfather and we didn't have the same last name, but I showed him my driver's license anyway. Acting real annoyed, I think I scared the guy, so he said he would open the door for me. I told him to give me the key, but the asshole insisted on opening it himself.

I stood in front of him as he opened the door because I wasn't sure what the deal was with Alex. I assumed she had passed out from drinking the night before and maybe had her headphones on and couldn't hear. The manager opened the door, and I stepped in front of him as he tried to look in. I don't think he saw her, but he was real suspicious. I took the key out, put it in my pocket, and locked the door behind me. I figured if that little bastard called the cops, I would be out of there as soon as I found out what the deal was with Alex.

I turned back toward Alex and realized what the problem was. There was an empty pill bottle on the floor next to her. There was a puddle of puke near her head, so I rolled her out of it and checked her pulse on her carotid artery. I could barely feel it, but it was there. She was breathing real shallow. Of course the first thing

I did was smack her on each side of the cheek. Shit, that was the movies taking over.

"Alex. Alex! Wake up, baby," I said as I shook her gently.

I lifted her eyelids, and her eyes were rolled back. At this point, I was pretty fucking scared. I ran to the door, and the manager was slowly walking back to his office.

"Hey!"

He turned and looked at me with a *what do you want* attitude.

"Call nine one one, and ask for an ambulance. She needs to go to the hospital," I shouted.

"What's wrong with her?" he asked.

"Just call them damn it!" Stupid bastard.

I went back in and picked Alex up to get her to walk. I really didn't know what else to do. No dice. She wasn't walking anywhere. I laid her on the couch and went and grabbed the ice bucket from the refrigerator. I lifted her shirt and put the ice on her stomach and chest. I also poured some inside her panties. I was grasping at anything that could bring her around. I held her head against my chest and was talking to her.

"Alex, please wake up." Her eyelids fluttered. "That's a girl. Wake up, Alex."

You could tell she was trying to open her eyes, but whatever had control of her was not allowing that. All of a sudden, she threw up all over my shirt. Fuck! My first reaction was to slap the shit out of her, but I held that back as well as the instinct for me to follow suit and throw up as well.

I set her head down and pulled off my shirt, and that's when she threw up again. This time, it was much more. She began gagging, and I turned her head to make sure she could get it all out. Then the tears started, and she began wailing, holding on to me. She was crying, choking, coughing, and wailing incoherently, but she was holding me around my neck tight.

"Please. Please help me," she said, but she still hadn't opened her eyes. The ice was starting to melt and fall out of her shirt as she struggled to sit up.

"Lie down, Alex. Help is on the way," I told her.

She relaxed a bit just as the EMT tech walked in the door. Of course a cop was right behind him. I looked around and picked up the pill bottle and put it in my pocket.

"I'll take over," the tech said.

The officer was standing behind us and was trying to assess the situation. As I walked away from Alex, he followed me.

"What's her problem?" he asked me.

"Really bad stomach flu or maybe something she ate."

"We got a call that someone broke in."

I looked behind the officer, and in the doorway was Manager Asshole.

"Look, no one broke in. The manager let me in. Here's the key," I said as I pulled it out of my pocket.

I explained the whole situation about why I was there, and by the time I got it all cleared up, Alex was in the ambulance.

"Hey, I want to go with her," I yelled.

I got in, sat next to Alex, and held her hand. I wanted to kiss her. I don't know why then, of all times. And I still don't know why it took her being dependent on me for a few minutes for me to fall in love. I suppose it must have been some kind of sickness; I don't know. That's what shrinks are for.

We got to the hospital, and I checked her in. I figured I was paying anyway, so I lied my way through most of the paper work. Jeez, they make it hard for anyone to be honest nowadays. They took her into the emergency room and worked on her, and I guess they pumped her stomach. Since I was the responsible party, the hospital sent in counseling services to talk to me. I wasn't her next of kin, but again had to lie to be able to help her out. Before I could check her out, I had to arrange for a counselor and then promise to get her rehab and all that shit.

Finally, about six hours later, I was able to go into her room. She was sleeping and hooked up to the IV. She really looked like the living dead now. Her pale skin was like an empty canvas against her blond hair. Her eyes were sunk deep into her sockets, leaving a black-eye look under each eye. And, yet, I found her to be amazingly beautiful. I held her hand. She opened her eyes and squeezed my hand, managing a slight smile. All that time, I was wondering if she felt the same. No way, Jackson. No way.

I called Carl, let him know what happened, and told him I would stay with her since all of her family lived in Kansas City. I slept in the chair that night, holding her hand all night. When I woke, she was looking at me. Looking at me more with curiosity than anything I guess.

"Why did you take care of me?" she asked.

"I guess because no one else was around to do it."

She smiled. "That makes sense. Thank you, Jackson. I'm sorry you had to see me like that."

I grinned and said, "No problem, Alex. You've never seen me at my worst."

We talked for about an hour and got to know each other a bit better. I really had only known her a couple of months. She was kind of a loner and didn't have a boyfriend or family here. I didn't pry or ask questions to find out what made her overdose. She didn't want to call her family, so I stayed with her until we checked her out of the hospital a couple of days later. I suggested that she stay at my place for a week, while she got things sorted out. She was agreeable, but she said after a week she was probably going to move back to Kansas City. I understood.

The first day was pretty intense. I caught her rummaging around in my medicine cabinet, and she had my Vicodin in her hands. I was pissed, and I yelled at her; she started crying. I had to lock up my liquor, my dope, and my pills. The next day was worse. I woke her up for breakfast. She got up and headed for where I was standing in the doorway and started screaming at me. I was stunned as nothing she screamed made sense. She slapped my face and started to attack me. I wasn't sure what the fuck had happened, but I wasn't equipped for this. That afternoon, I put her in rehab. Turns out she just recently started smoking crack, and the pills were just an additional vice she had just started.

It was a real sterile clinic, and the people there had years of experience in drug dependency issues. I talked to Alex for a few minutes before I left. She began crying again and apologized. The next thing I did was tell her I love her. She just looked at me with that puzzled look. You know, like, *What the hell?* I figured I scared her, so I kissed her on the forehead and walked away.

Two weeks later, I flew out to Kansas City. I remember taking a rose to see Alex. As I walked up to her, I was crying, and I set the rose on her chest. She looked so beautiful. She no longer had the living-dead-girl look. This time she was really dead, lying in a casket. She had hung herself that same night I left her in rehab. They found a note on the floor underneath her body that read, "I love you, too." I know one thing: this one hurt me the most. I can't believe I had let my guard down so fast. It just hurt. I needed something or someone to help me fill the void of that sting.

# CHAPTER 13

# IN LOVE, AGAIN?

*How beautiful and pleasant you are, O loved one, with*
*all your delights!*

*—Song of Solomon 7:6*

There was one morning I woke up, and it was different than most. I blinked and rubbed my eyes and noticed the sun was already up. I reached to touch Allison lying in bed next to me, but only emptiness filled the sheets where just a few hours earlier she had slept. Her perfume still lingered in my sheets.

I licked my lips to recall the taste of her kiss, but my morning cigarette had already fouled any remnants of the previous night. The Charlie Parker record was still on repeat and played softly to set a mood for two lovers who were no longer together. She had retreated to a place unknown to me. I sat on the edge of my bed and started wondering if maybe she had a husband or children. We'd never discussed it. I wouldn't have cared anyway.

It started in April, and I guess spring fever must have been in the air. I was sitting in this quaint little deli in midtown, eating by myself again. In walked this woman in her late twenties. She was a short, skinny woman with a cute boyish haircut. What hair she had was auburn with a three-inch streak of deep purple. As my curiosity stayed with her, I noticed she wore no makeup, and her nose was pierced with a small diamond in the left nostril.

She wore blue jeans that were riding low on her narrow hips, revealing the Joe Boxer lining of her underwear. She had on a white muscle shirt and an old red flannel shirt that was two sizes too big. The hostess walked her to a table next to mine, judging the young lady with her eyes the entire walk from the door. We nodded to each other and smiled.

After a few minutes of staring at the menu, I finally ordered the usual Rueben sandwich on rye with an extra side of pickles and a Dr Pepper. I looked over at the young woman and noticed she was fidgeting with the menu, trying to make up her mind.

She leaned over in my direction. "What did you order?"

I told her.

She smiled. "Is it good?"

I shrugged. "Works for me."

It was her smile. Her smile was shaped like some strange frown with her full lips. And she had the most beautiful sea-green eyes that stunned me. She placed her order, same as mine, as I sat there fantasizing about kissing her lips.

When I was finished with my meal, I got up, nodded, and smiled at the young lady. I walked to the counter to pay and told the cashier to add her bill to mine.

"Do you know her?"

"Nope, it just makes me feel like I'm not eating alone," I replied.

He shrugged and rang it up, and I paid. I walked out to the parking garage and was almost to my car. "Hey!" I heard this high pitch voice yell. "I didn't get to thank you. I'm Allison." I was standing by my car.

"Hello, Allison. I'm Ramsey, but you can call me Ram."

She walked right into my personal space and looked up at me. "Ram, like the sheep? Ha-ha! Do you always buy strangers lunch, Ram?"

"Yes, Allison, like the sheep, only better looking. And it doesn't seem like we're strangers anymore," I joked.

She was biting her bottom lip a bit and just standing there, quizzically looking at me. Then without any notice, she walked right up, stood on her tiptoes, and kissed me full on the mouth. She pressed her lips against mine, and we opened our mouths and explored each other. I picked her up, and she wrapped her legs around me as I fell back on my car hood and sat down.

Here we go again. It seemed so right. With some further introduction, I scrapped work that day, and we went to my apartment and made love. She wound up staying two days and nights. But as the sun was coming up on the third day, as if she were some kind of vampire, she left, walking out of my house and disappearing.

Two weeks later, on a Thursday, I was sitting in the diner when Allison walked in. She looked in my direction and put her finger to her lips as if to shush me. I was confused because no one was with her, and I didn't know why she would blow me off. She pointed in my direction to the hostess, asking to sit at the table next to mine.

When she sat down, I started to say something.

"Shhh!" she hissed, wrinkling her forehead. "What did you order?"

I was feeling a déjà vu coming on as I told her.

"Is it good?" she asked.

I smiled. "It works for me."

During the meal, she never once looked at me, and I was freaked out. Actually, I was getting a bit angry about the whole ordeal. I got up and paid for my meal. As I walked out, I turned to look at her, and she looked away. I shrugged and walked out. I stopped by the paper stand and bought a pack of cigarettes. By the time I got to my car, Allison was sitting on my hood with that crazy frown smile.

"Why didn't you buy my lunch, Ram?"

I laughed. "Are you a total wacko? Where did you go that day?"

She said, "Does it really matter? I'm here now."

We kissed again, on the hood of my car, and again we went to my house and made love for two days and nights. She left again before the sun came up on the third day.

We had been doing this same crazy routine now every two weeks on Thursday for almost six months now. We never talked about anything except books, music, or movies. We drank tequila, smoked cigarettes, and shared our bodies together, but Allison was still a stranger to me. Allison had left again that day. But that day was different. I had fallen in love with a stranger.

Yes, that day was different from most. I heard the door open, and Allison walked back to the bedroom and asked, "Are you going to get up, lazy bones?" She had a bag of groceries in her arms, and she was smiling that beautiful upside-down-smile thing that she did. "Stay here, Ram. I'll bring us some breakfast." She made us a tray of orange juice, coffee, a couple of cups of mango slices, and wheat toast. I'll never forget it. She set the tray on the bed, took off her clothes, and slipped under the sheet.

We lay there in bed and ate breakfast. It was real relaxing.

"I'm really glad you came back, Allison," I told her.

"Me, too, Ram." She grinned.

"I need to tell you something, Allison," I responded.

"Great. Here it comes," she said while rolling her eyes and grinning.

"I don't want you to leave again," I continued. "I want you to move in with me. I'm falling in love with you."

There it was. It was out. I hadn't said that to anyone since Liz. I waited for her reaction. Those beautiful sea-green eyes had the answer as they lit up.

"I want to stay, Ram. I really do," she said as I waited for the "but" shoe to drop.

Her face got real serious, and she closed her eyes. It looked like she was really thinking about her next line. I must have looked panicked and hurt.

She opened her eyes and laughed. "Ha! You should see your face!"

I think I went from hurt to pissed and was about to speak when she asked, "So when do I move in?"

Yep, that was my little Allison all right. Always the cocky smart-ass. She had me going. We both laughed, and she moved in that weekend. I prayed to God that it would work out because I really did love her. She calmed me.

There's something to be said about a commitment that is built on sex. They don't work out that well. After a year of living together, we started getting bored in the bedroom. Don't get me wrong. I really still loved her, and we had a lot of fun together. We even made a trip to Costa Rica and had a hell of a week taking in the jungles and the beaches. I don't know if it was our twelve-year age gap or what, but it just didn't feel right. Even after a year, it was as if we were still strangers.

# CHAPTER 14
# CRAZY NINA

*Let all that you do be done in love.*

*—John 4:8*

One night we decided to go out and buy something to help us out, so I drove us to a twenty-four-hour porno store. I went in along and was rifling through the "Best of the Best Video Selection." Catherine Wheel was singing "Black Metallic" on the speakers above me, and I was thinking how fucked up things really were for me again. Finally, I saw something that might make her happy. Allison seemed to really get worked up over lesbian films. There was a time when just making out with her would do the trick. I guess it was either boredom or my new portly shape. Who the fuck knows why two people who used to be crazy about each other finally get to the point where being away from each other is the only way to salvage a relationship. Whatever. Lesbian film it was. I looked across the place. I thought, *Man, look at all those toys.* That place was all about self-serve.

I looked over the crowd in the store and wondered if I was really like them. Lost souls, couples, singles, men, women, lesbians, gays, freaks, drug addicts, businessmen—all looking for a companion on film. I took the film to the cashier, and she eyed me over, trying to get my story. *Man, she's a hot one,* I thought. A PIB, person in black. And she had more body piercing and art than I've ever seen on a woman. Her hair was dyed pinkish purple, and she had dark mascara, black lipstick, and black fingernail polish. She had on a tank top, exposing purple bra straps.

What I'd have given to have left this place with her instead of my Allison waiting for me in the car.

"It's not for me," I said.

"No shit?" she sarcastically said with a smile. "I'm a virgin," she continued.

A guy at the gay-film section looked up at us and laughed.

"Well, let me know if you ever want to change that" was all I could think to say.

She gave me the total, and I gave her a twenty.

"No way you could handle it," she bantered back.

A lady in the adult-toy department was craning her neck to hear us.

"I'm serious. I like your look," I told her.

She gave me my change without saying anything. I started to walk away with a confused look on my face. Shot down, again. I was almost to the door.

"Sir, don't forget your receipt."

I went back, and she pressed it into my hand, looked me in the eyes, and smiled. Whatever. I was very confused. I put the receipt in my pocket. Allison was in the car, waiting patiently. That girl had worked me up. I liked her look and damned sure liked that sassy bullshit she was giving me. We got home, switched on the video, and watched those talented ladies do things that only women can understand. We started making out. Sure, that did it. Allison was tuned up and was ready to go. After that hottie in the video store, I was too. We both got what we wanted out of the deal. I couldn't stop thinking about the porno-store girl. So I guess I had my own images in my mind.

The next morning, I threw my jeans on and went into the kitchen to make coffee. It was a bit chilly, and I put my hands in my pockets to warm them up. I felt a piece of paper in my pockets. It was the receipt. I took it out and looked at it. Well, I'll be damned. On the back she had written a name and phone number and drawn a frowning face: "Nina—653-6969." Ha, very funny. I figured it was a fake number, but I put it back on my pocket just in case I decided to call it later. Allison came in all blurry eyed, and we sat in complete silence and drank our coffee. Yep, this drill was just about done. I couldn't stop thinking about Nina and the phone number. I got ready for work and headed out the door.

Work sucked, as usual, but when lunch came around, I called the number.

"Hello?" a woman's voice answered after three rings.

"Is Nina there?" I asked.

"Hey, big guy, I was wondering if you were going to call."

"How did you know it was me?" I asked.

She said nothing. There was a long pause.

"Hello?" I thought the call dropped.

"Did you call for a reason?" she asked.

"You gave me your number, remember," I said kind of irritated.

"Look, I gave you that number for a reason. Now, let's try this again," she said.

Ah, the fucking light bulb went off. I guess it was like that with her. So I asked "When can we meet?"

She said, "Now, that's better. How about in an hour?"

I whined. "But I have to work."

She hung up. Wow, now this shit was getting better all the time. She was all business. I dialed her back, and she answered, "Look, I don't have time for bullshit. You seem like a nice guy, and I don't do nice guys. So you need to make up your mind what it is you want."

I said, "Look, I get it. See you in an hour."

I got directions to her place and headed over to see her.

I pulled into a driveway of a really well-kept Victorian-style home. The yard was manicured, and the outside of the house had hints of fresh paint. It was in the older section of town that had been revitalized with all the old hippies buying up property and restoring the old houses. I rang the doorbell. Nina opened the door with a cigarette hanging out of her mouth and was dressed in the same outfit she had on last night. She said nothing and walked away, leaving the door open.

I walked in. "What? No kiss hello?"

Nina turned around. "Funny guy."

I shut the door. She walked toward me and pushed me in the chest hard. "I don't like funny guys."

Right then I thought about walking back out. Who knew what she was up to?

"You want a kiss, huh? Is that it? Big fucking baby wants a kiss?"

I started to laugh. She reached up slowly to kiss me. I put my arms around her, and she bit my fucking lip. Hard. I could taste blood.

"Forget this shit. I don't play like this." I angrily pushed her away from me.

"You fucking pussy! That's what I thought. I said you couldn't handle it," she yelled.

I had my hand on the doorknob. I couldn't leave. I walked back over to her, grabbed her by her ass cheeks with both hands, picked her up to my level, and kissed her hard. I pushed my tongue into her mouth, feeling the ball of her pierced tongue flicking against my tongue. I could feel her double lip rings hard against my mouth, and it hurt. It hurt good. God, I could feel everything. I was back to life.

She was sucking on my tongue and pulling my hair hard at the same time. I couldn't tell what hurt and what felt good. I never had such a crazy sensation in my life. I put her down. She pushed me onto the couch and climbed up into my lap, tearing my shirt along the way. I tore the rest of it off with no regard for later consequences. She was fumbling with my belt and pants, while I pulled all of her top garments off. As I figured, both of her nipples were pierced with large gauge rings. We became animals in the jungle. Biting, sucking, kissing, moaning, screaming, cussing, pulling, and pushing. We fucked. We didn't make love. We didn't procreate. We fucked hard, fast, and long. It was one of the best times I've ever had doing just that.

When we finished, we lay on the couch, her on top of me. I could feel her heartbeat against my chest. Man, I liked this Nina. *Where the hell has she been?* It was as if I was dying, and she had given me CPR and rescued me. She got up on her elbows on my chest. It kind of hurt, but we just looked into each other's eyes. I never noticed eyes like hers. She had a black ring on the outside of her irises of green. She kissed me. A bit softer this time. She smiled and stuck her tongue out at me, flicking her tongue ring. My little pin cushion. Damn, I liked this girl. She started kissing my chest and gently nibbling my nipples. Everything had slowed down. We were building up for round two, and I had a feeling it was going to be better than the first. She turned around, still lying on top of me, and we fucked again; we finished exhausted, still laying in that position.

That day was a great day! Later that night, I was thinking about it pretty much all night. Allison and I were sitting on the couch watching a movie. I was thinking about Nina and smiling, and Allison asked me what I was thinking. I recovered quickly and told her I wanted to make love to her right then. I was like an animal again. I was on top of her in no time. Allison responded in kind, and whatever we had been bored with was rekindled. I pulled her pants down and mine, and we fucked hard on the couch. We rolled off and smoked a cigarette. We didn't say much, but it was clear that we were better.

But as it goes with me, a taste was not good enough. I had to see Nina again. I had left her house without either of us saying anything about the future.

# CHAPTER 15
# ALLISON MEETS NINA

*For this reason God gave them up to dishonorable*
*passions. For their women exchanged natural relations for*
*those that are contrary to nature.*

*—Romans 1:26*

I was lying in bed half-asleep, half dreaming about Nina. I was remembering seeing the tails of a leopard and a panther, one on
each of her butt cheeks, as she was facing away from me. The animals were both tattooed, one on each side of her navel, running
across her side and across her back with their tails hanging down
to her buttocks. The tails met together in the middle and formed
a smile. Strange. I think I was laughing in my sleep when I felt this
*whump* on the bed next to me!

"Wake the fuck up!" Allison was screaming.

I was stirring, trying to figure out what was going on. The next
blow caught me in my ribs. It knocked the breath out of me, and I
painfully rolled out of bed on Allison's side, rather quickly, before

the next *whump* caught the middle of the bed. Wide awake now, I looked up to see Allison holding my seven iron that I kept under my side of the bed for protection. She had a crazy look on her face and was swinging it over and over, hitting nothing but air as I danced around the other side of bed. I figured I was in some deep shit and should better find out what pissed her off before she threw the club.

"Who's Nina?" she asked.

Oh, fuck. I realized I had just emptied my pockets when I came in last night and threw everything, including the porn-store receipt with Nina's number, on my nightstand.

"Did she scratch you up like that? Are you fucking her?" she quizzed in her loudest screams. I think Allison had all the answers right about now.

I was holding my ribs, trying to catch my breath, and thinking how stupid I really was. Nina had clawed my back and my chest. I had a shirt on when Allison and I made love on the couch the night before. I had taken my shirt off when I got to bed, and I made no effort to hide it. I figured I would deal with the consequences later, and later was now. Before I could say anything, the seven iron flew across the bed and hit me on my forearm right as I lifted it up to protect my head. A second slower, and I would have been out. Damn, that hurt.

Allison started screaming, "Get your shit, and get out! No, forget that. You don't get anything. Get the fuck out right now!"

I was about to give her that *Allison I can explain* bullshit, but I knew that would make things worse. I started gathering up some clothes as Allison stared at me.

"Say something, you fucking asshole!"

Here I was naked, holding my ribs, scratched up, with a fucking lip that was still swollen from Nina biting it yesterday, and guilty as hell. What could I possibly say?

"Allison, yesterday was the culmination of my entire sexual life all rolled up into one giant sexual experience. And you know what, I'd do it again."

That caught her off guard. Allison stared at me. "Is that what last night was?" she asked. "Were you thinking of her and fucking me?" she was still yelling. She didn't know whether to pick something up and throw it or cry. She was shaking.

I started walking around the side of the bed to comfort her.

"Don't you dare!" she screamed. "Just leave."

While I was putting on my clothes, I was gasping for air and trying to get the pain in my ribs to stop. I definitely believed she broke a couple. I could hear Allison dialing her cell phone. I walked in to see who she was calling. I knew already.

"Nina!" Allison looked at the phone. I laughed to myself.

"That bitch hung up on me!" she said.

"That's a shock" was all I could think to say as I started to walk down the hall to the bedroom to get dressed.

"Don't you dare walk out on me," Allison screamed as she threw her cell phone down the hall at me. I was surprised it didn't shatter as it bounced onto the floor and sat there spinning.

"You'd better settle the fuck down!" I screamed at her as I ran down the hall after her.

She stood her ground. "What are you going to do, hit me? Come on, asshole, hit me! I'll have your ass in jail so fast."

I grabbed her in a bear hug to keep her arms pinned and lifted her off the ground. I pulled her into my chest and kissed her. She was struggling, trying to kick my balls. I held my mouth against her and finally she relented. She started kissing me back.

She pulled back. "Is that what you did with Nina?"

I pushed my head forward and kept kissing her. Finally, she relaxed, and we began kissing passionately as I carried her into the bedroom. I tossed her on the bed and sat on top of her, still kissing her.

"You want to know what I did with Nina?" I asked as I bit her lip hard. "That's just a taste."

God, I had never seen Allison turned on as much as she was now. I ripped her nightshirt and tore it off. She slapped me hard and was going for the other cheek when I pinned her arms back on the bed. She spit in my face. That was the closest I ever came to slapping Allison in the time I'd known her. It must have shown on my face because she reacted with an *oh shit* look.

She was trying to buck me off, and I bent forward and began kissing her breasts. She was losing the fight. Her rapid breathing from fighting so hard began slowing down. Her breasts were always so sensitive. She started moaning.

"Call me Nina. Say it!"

I let go of her arms. I figured I was safe now. "Nina, oh, Nina." I obeyed.

She reached up and was slowly stroking my hair. I kept going back from one breast to the other. Suddenly, she pulled my hair with both of her hands. I swear I heard some rip out.

"Don't you ever call me that again."

Man, I think I'd just found myself in the middle of a fucked-up situation that I created.

"Allison! Allison, damn, that hurts," I whined.

She let go. "Get off me," she said.

"Don't hit me again, and I will," I said as I flipped off her.

She got on top of me now. She began tracing the scratches on my chest left by Nina. "She did this to you?"

I had said enough already, so I didn't say anything. She mounted me, and we made love, slow, staring into each other's eyes. Nothing was said; we were just engulfed in passion.

We finished, and she rolled off. "Call her and tell her you just fucked me," Allison said.

"No, I'm not calling her again," I told her.

"No, I'm serious. Call her," Allison demanded.

I picked my phone up off the floor, looked up her name, and called her. I had already put on speed dial after one call.

"Hey, stud," Nina answered.

Allison took the phone away from me and gently whispered, "Nina, he just fucked me just like he fucked you."

I could hear Nina's reply over the phone. "I doubt that, hon." Nina hung up the phone.

"Call her back," Allison said.

"Look, Allison, I don't know what you want out of this. Let's drop it. I'll leave if you want, but let it go."

She though a minute and said, "Then what, let you move in with her? No way. Let's go see her. I want to know what she looks like."

I pleaded and begged to make Allison drop this shit, but she wouldn't.

We drove up to Nina's house. "Wow, nice place," Allison commented. I rang the doorbell, while Allison stood off to the side. No answer. I rang again, and this time Nina opened the door. God, she had changed her look in one day. This time her hair was jet black with a purple streak running right down the middle like a skunk. She was wearing a white tank top with no bra and black leather shorts with thigh-high lace-up boots on. Fashion queen she was not.

As she walked away, I noticed two tattoos I hadn't seen yesterday, a "69" on each of her wrists. And again she turned her back on me and walked away, leaving me to walk in. Allison beat me to it. "Hey, bitch!"

Nina turned back and faced Allison. She smiled. "I figured you'd be coming. Just couldn't stand it, could you? You had to see what he wanted so bad that he would risk you." Nina continued. "Take a good look, hon."

She pulled off her tank top, exposing her breasts, and Allison could only gasp. God, what a body Nina had.

"Let's go, Allison." I was afraid Allison was going to start shit and get her assed kicked. Nina was no woman to fuck with.

"Shut up, stud! You're not in this," Nina yelled.

She was right. This wasn't about me.

Nina started toward Allison. "You're the girl who wanted stud here to get a lesbian movie, right? Huh?"

Allison was frozen. She didn't know whether to turn and run or get ready for a fight. She looked over at me. I shrugged my shoulders. That reminded me that the pain in my ribs was still there. While Allison looked over at me, Nina had gotten closer and grabbed Allison's face.

"I'm talking to you, Allison. Do you really want to know what it's like?" She kissed Allison, gently.

Allison moaned. I could see a tear forming in the corner of her eye. Allison opened her mouth and welcomed Nina's kisses. Gentle, deep, wet kisses. I thought I was going to pass out. Most men dreamed about this, and here I was, finally getting to be a part of it.

Allison put her hand up and touched one of Nina's nipple rings. She started gently pulling and playing with it. Nina lifted Allison's blouse and undid her bra, exposing her breasts. Allison was shaking now.

Nina went to the floor, kissing Allison's pelvic region through her pants. She was biting her all over her legs and midsection as she undid her jeans. Allison pulled Nina's head closer and began gyrating her hips into Nina's face. Both of them were moaning now.

Nina pulled off her shorts and was naked, except for those tall boots. She stood up and pulled Allison's naked body against hers. They continued kissing as I began walking toward them. Nina held up her hand as if to halt me. I understood; I went and sat on the couch and watched them. It was beautiful.

Two women, softly, gently making love to each other as only they understood how to do it. The smell of woman in the air, watching two beautiful bodies pressed together, moving in unison. I'd finally had enough and began undressing. I lay naked next to them on the floor and watched. A bit later, we were all lying on the floor, kissing and holding each other. We collapsed in a heap with Allison's head on my right shoulder and Nina's on my left shoulder.

I was exhausted from the two solid days with those two. My ribs were killing me, and I hurt in places I never knew existed. Allison couldn't get that smile off her face, and Nina came home with us. I just hoped things never got weird. But they did.

# CHAPTER 16

# FOR THE LOVE OF PABLO NERUDA

*Be sober minded; be watchful. Your adversary the devil prowls around like a roaring lion, seeking someone to devour.*

*—1 Peter 5:8*

On one of my trips to Costa Rica, I had purchased a book at an airport bookstore. The book was titled *The Complete Works of Pablo Neruda*. Pablo Neruda was a Chilean poet and had a way with words that made up some of the most romantic poems I'd ever read. Allison and I had always liked the same things, like books and movies, but with her being distracted by Nina lately, it was apparent she wasn't interested in anything that I liked anymore. I had taken an interest in reading it again. I had been learning Spanish the past few years, so I figured I would read some to her in Spanish.

So one night when Nina had gone back to her house, I called Allison into the room and began to read one of our favorite poems from the book in Spanish.

"Really, Ram?" she asked. "Are you really doing this now?"

"I really thought we could—"

"Not tonight, Ram!" she yelled.

I took the book and walked, dejected, out onto the back deck and began reading those beautifully sculpted words, letting them take me away. Still, I longed for someone to enjoy the words with me. I tried again the next night with the same results. We never got to read together again, and three weeks later, we broke up. She moved in with Nina, and I guess they lived happily ever after.

I was really heartbroken over Allison. It was all my fault. I never should have fucked around with Nina, and as fun as all of that shit was, I regretted it. I pretty much took the book everywhere I went and never missed a chance to read it. One night while I was out of town on business, I was bored of just sitting in my hotel room. I think it was about six months since Allison left, and I was pretty lonely. I was reading the Pablo Neruda book and was longing for some company, someone who would get it. So, as desperation would have it, I began fumbling through the yellow pages looking for any type of service that could send someone to just sit here and enjoy these words with me. Finally, I settled on an advertisement that read, "Sophisticated, Well-Read Ladies, We Speak Several Languages." I debated with myself for several minutes and finally decided to call.

A sweet voice on the other end of the line asked, "What can we do for you?"

"What do you do?" I asked, but I already knew the answer.

"Pretty much anything you want us to, darling," she replied in a sexy voice.

I quickly hung up the phone. *Goddamned chicken!* I thought. I really had turned into a pussy.

I waited a few minutes until the embarrassment wore off, and I called her back.

"Hi there. What happened?" she asked.

*Oh, great, she recognized my voice,* I thought. "I had another call." I lied.

"So can we do something for you tonight?" she asked.

I said, "Sure, do you have anyone there who can come over and read aloud from a wonderful book of poetry I have?"

"We sure do," she answered. "Would you like a blonde or a brunette?"

I thought for a minute. Since I was choosing, and Neruda was Chilean and Spanish was the language, I might as well ask for someone who speaks Spanish.

"Do you have a Latina?" I asked.

"No, hon, sorry I don't," she replied.

"OK, send over a brunette I guess," I said with a hint of dejection in my voice.

She got the room number and specifics and said she would call me back in a few minutes to confirm. I hung up the phone, opened my book, and began to read.

Dear God, what have I done? The phone rang. A young lady's voice was on the other end.

"Ramsey, I'm in the lobby. May I come up?"

"Yes," I answered.

"Room thirty-three thirty-three, right?" she quizzed.

"Uh, that's right, thirty-three thirty-three. I'll be here," I replied nervously and hung up the phone.

"Oh my God! What a fucking loser! Where else would you be?" I asked myself.

There was a faint knock on the door. I opened the door, and a young lady in her early twenties stood there looking at me. She had a pretty face with dark brown eyes, but her eyes were dead. No spark at all. I should have sent her away then. She was wearing a pink tube dress with black heels. I realized there was a mistake with the ad I responded to. For fear of being judgmental, she was quite too young to be a "Sophisticated, Well-Read Lady."

"Hi, I'm Mary Ann," she said. "First time?" She continued. "Well, I guess Monica explained it to you over the phone. There will be a one-hundred-seventy-five-dollar processing fee. We take Visa or MasterCard."

I didn't hear the rest of what she was explaining about tips and such as I was feeling a bit faint and had a sick feeling in my stomach. This wasn't exactly what I had in mind for the night. I gave her the money for the processing fee, and she smiled and asked, "OK, Ram, what now?"

I was used to being in charge when it came to women, but I must have looked like a fucking retard because she gave me the weirdest look as I was still clutching my Pablo Neruda book throughout all of this.

"I wondered if you wouldn't mind reading from this book?" I asked.

"What is it?" she asked, obviously uninterested.

"Why, it's Pablo Neruda," I said proudly, "a Chilean poet."

As if she had a fucking clue, I thought. She had this really blank look on her face.

"Why don't you get comfortable, and I'll do the same," she said.

She went into the bathroom, and I sat on the bed and began reading again.

She came out of the bathroom wearing a short brown see-through nightgown. I watched her approach me and could see her large round areolas through the gown. As she got closer, I could smell a musk type of perfume on her. I have to admit, I was somewhat excited but realized this was not the place or the time.

"I thought you were going to get comfortable," she said.

"I am comfortable," I said, still clutching the book.

"Look, I don't have all night," her tone changed. "I can model for you, I can dance for you, I can strip for you, and I can do anything you want if the tip is right. So what is it you want?"

I would say the next emotion I had was fear. She scared the shit out of me. She went from being a Bambi look-alike to a real uptight bitch.

"I was told by the lady on the phone you would read to me," I whined.

"Look, you seem like a nice guy. I'm just not going to sit here and waste my time reading to a guy." She continued. "If you will strip down, I will dance for you, and you can get off. How's that?"

*Fuck that,* I thought. *I can get off by myself.* "That's OK. Never mind," I said.

I pulled one hundred dollars out of my wallet and said, "Here's for your trouble. Sorry it didn't work out."

She went back into the bathroom and changed. She came out, made a phone call from my hotel phone, and left without saying good-bye. I locked the door behind her and turned and faced the empty room. I had never, before or since that moment, felt so horrible about my life. I had one of those moments. You know, where you sob so deep into the pillow that you pray you smother.

I think, during that fucking crying episode, I realized one thing. I really just wanted to be loved. But all I did was fuck that up. How could I have ever stooped this low and have called someone to read to me? I was sick to my stomach. *Goddamn it, why can't I just read to myself like a normal person? Why isn't there this perfect person out there for me? There must be a woman for me who loves the words. The words of true love, hope, peace, and truth. A life with someone like this can't just be a fantasy.*

I used that night as a lesson to remind me how low I could sink to find someone to connect with. I kept the receipt from that night with me at all times. Sometimes I would just pull the receipt out and stare at it, remembering that night, my punishment I suppose. I also put away the Pablo Neruda book and put away dreams of true love, hope, passion, or anything else that went with a relationship. I never told anyone of that night and vowed to stop looking for that person to share those special feelings with. A couple of years of drinking, drugging, sexual relationships, and self-loathing went by, and my yearning returned. I decided to take a trip to clear my mind and get away from it all. I had no intention of returning.

I flew to Costa Rica and found a quiet little village tucked away in the jungle. I always figured if I ever ran away, this would be where I would go. I had been to Costa Rica before but not this remote. I suppose I was running away. I had only packed a few things with me. One, of course, was my Pablo Neruda book.

I tried reading it on the plane over, but quickly became bored. It wasn't the same. I just couldn't capture the same excitement and other feelings again. The guilt over the incident at the hotel was still haunting me I suppose. I got off the plane, caught a bus, and settled into my room. I had to admit, the country was more beautiful than I remembered. I picked up my book, went over to a cantina, and ordered a bottle of tequila. *Nothing like a little self-medication to cure what ails you,* I figured.

I studied an old couple who I figured for locals in the corner of the cantina. The old man was reading a San Jose newspaper, while his wife was muttering something to him in Spanish. He appeared not to hear her, which only irritated her. I figure the old man was in his midsixties, and he had a deep scar across his cheek that ran down past his jaw to his neck. As I watched him, my imagination took over, and I created a knife fight in my mind where this man must have gotten cut.

His wife was probably a few years younger than him, and she still had a pretty complexion. She had looked at me when I first walked in and flashed a beautiful smile with life still left in her dark eyes. Her once jet-black hair was showing signs of gray. She wore a long black skirt and white blouse with a black patterned jacket.

She said something to her husband once again in Spanish, and he put down his paper and sighed. He looked at her this time with interest as she spoke to him. They glanced in my direction, and it was making me a bit uneasy since I was the stranger here. Then the old man got up and went outside for a few minutes. The woman smiled at me again. I raised a glass of tequila in her direction as if to toast her and smiled back. Soon, the husband came back, sat down, and continued reading his newspaper.

I kept thinking how odd that situation was, but since I was a stranger in town, I should just accept it, keep my eyes open, and go on minding my own business. I began to feel the warmth of the tequila.

I went to the bar and asked the bartender in my best Spanish, "Marlboro lights *y cerillos por favor.*"

"Yes sir," the bartender replied back in broken English.

I took the cigarettes and matches, went back to his table, and sat down. I poured myself another tequila and lit a cigarette. I opened the Pablo Neruda book and began reading.

I took a long puff from the cigarette and swallowed the tequila. I went back to reading, and all of a sudden, I heard a woman's voice read in perfect Spanish, reading the exact same passage I was reading.

I quickly looked up and gasped to the point of almost hyperventilating. Man, this woman scared the shit out of me and embarrassed me all in one moment.

The woman who was reading over my shoulder put her arm around me and said in perfect English with a hint of a Spanish accent, "I didn't mean to startle you. I love Pablo Neruda," she continued.

She was a very pretty woman, and I figured her as a native as well, and the way the old couple was grinning, maybe related to them. She wore a long-sleeve cotton shirt unbuttoned to the third button. She had on a long dark riding skirt and riding boots. She had her black hair pulled back into a tight bun. When I recovered, I finally asked her to sit down. I motioned to the bartender for another glass. He walked over, smiling, but with a puzzled look on his face, and set another clean glass on the table. Remembering the hotel incident I still hadn't forgotten, I figured, *Here we go again.*

"I'm Isabel," she said.

I watched her watch me. I started noticing things about her, like the scar on her chin, the reflections in her black eyes, and the way her lips curved ever so slightly to reveal her smile. I introduced myself to her and said I was from Texas. That was a real crowd pleaser as she told the old couple I was from Texas. They didn't even look up. I laughed and made a joke about no cowboy boots or hat. She laughed. Oh, God, that laugh—it was so sincere and alive. I made some joke about me running away, and she became serious.

"So, why are you running away?" she asked.

My mouth fell open, and the cigarette I was lighting fell out of my mouth. "I'm sorry?" I asked.

"Why would you want to run away? Are you a criminal?"

I tried my best to come up with an answer, but all I could muster was, "Let's just say things didn't work out for me at home."

We got into this long discussion about marriage, kids, job, and the usual stuff. Except with her, she seemed really interested. We sat there talking until dusk. I found out she was in her thirties, engaged once to an American, and had no kids. As she mentioned, she, too, loved Pablo Neruda, and as it turned out, she had the same book I did stowed away in her bag.

We waved at the bartender, and he gave us a puzzled look and waved back. We left the cantina and went for a walk, still talking about our lives as if we were trying to tell each other everything in one night. Nothing was shallow about Isabel. She wanted to know everything about me and wanted me to know everything about her. Time stopped for me that night. I figured that I had met that one person—you know, that one who you realize you'd better not ever let get away.

When we stopped walking, we found ourselves in front of her house. I felt a little uneasy going in with her because I didn't know if someone was going to knife me in the dark or what. You know all those stupid stories that somehow come up at the weirdest times. Anyway, I went in, and she fed me some kind of pasta dish with red wine. I felt like I had known her forever.

She leaned into me and kissed me. I swear she must have pasted honey all over her lips as all I could taste was sweet. I had no idea how long we made out. I was hungry for this beautiful woman. She grabbed my hand and led me into her bedroom. Watching her take down her hair was an event. My stomach got butterflies. I know right then I fell in love with her. Oh, yes, folks, the first night. We made love. It was so right, and we were so comfortable with each other. I felt like my life was finally complete. I would never go back home as long as I had Isabel.

The next day, I woke in Isabel's bedroom. She was already up making breakfast. I walked in, put my arm around her waist, and kissed her. Something was already different. I looked into her eyes, and the fire was gone. I felt like something hit me in the pit of my stomach.

"Are you OK?" I asked.

She was avoiding eye contact as she put the breakfast down in front of me. "Eat, and then you need to leave."

Fuck that. I felt myself getting pissed off. "What the hell happened?" I asked.

"Nothing. I have a busy day," she answered.

"Can I at least see you later?"

All she could mutter was, "We'll see."

I went back to my room and pondered over what the hell had happened. I read the Pablo Neruda book some more but could not calm down. Was I just being used? I went into the cantina where the old couple was still hanging around in the corner reading the newspaper.

I walked over to them and asked, "*Donde esta* Isabel?"

They looked up, startled. "*Que senor?*"

"Isabel, *la mujer de ayer.*" I was trying to figure out where Isabel was.

"Isabel *esta muerto.*"

Dead? Bullshit. Now I figured they were having fun with me.

I started yelling. "Isabel's not dead, goddamn it!" The old woman started crying, and the old man was upset as hell. The bartender came from around the bar and asked me in English what my problem was.

I told him about meeting Isabel in the cantina the day before. The bartender said he had not seen anyone else sitting with me and I had been reading from a book aloud. Since I wasn't bothering anyone, he figured he would leave me alone. I felt pretty sick, and I figured they were still playing a joke on me, but the couple was obviously upset.

I asked the bartender, "Then who the hell is Isabel then? Are you saying I sat there with a ghost?"

He began to tell me a story of a young woman named Isabel, the daughter of the old couple in the corner. How she had met a man from Texas in this same cantina five years ago to the day. They fell in love and were going to be married here in Costa Rica later that year. Her fiancé went back to the States to make arrangements to start living in Costa Rica. He was killed in a car accident on the way back to the airport. Isabel, heartbroken, took a walk down to the beach, walked into the water, and drowned. Although there were witnesses, her body was never recovered.

No fucking way this was happening.

"Are you saying that I talked, walked, ate with, and made love to a ghost?" I asked the bartender again.

He said, "Some say, they see her walking, with the same book you have under her arm, once a month looking for her lover."

I walked outside and threw up. I couldn't believe it. It was a story only Hollywood would come up with. I felt like I was being set up for some stupid-ass Costa Rican joke. I went back to my room and got really fucked up, trying to make this shit go away.

The next day, hungover from the night before, I went back into the cantina, and the old couple watched me intently as I sat down at my table. The old man had something in his hand and walked over to my table. He had the same Pablo Neruda book.

"*Este fue el libro de* Isabel."

It was Isabel's book. He gave it to me.

I opened it up and read the inscription: "To Isabel, with all my love, Jackson."

I sat at the table and cried as Isabel put her hand on my shoulders and began reading from the book in Spanish. No one saw her but me. I finally found my one true love, and she was reading me Pablo Neruda.

I booked the flight home. I realized I needed to go back to the States because this episode made me realize, with all of my life of drinking and drugging, I had to get some real help. I was seeing things, and this Isabel thing had really hurt.

A Christian friend of mine, who had remained a friend even though he knew my life and my lifestyle, referred me to a Christian counselor. In the first session with the counselor, I couldn't even get past the initial greeting. He opened with a prayer and asked God to help with the session so I could see where God could work in my life. I broke down. I spent almost an hour crying. Jim, my counselor, just put his hand on my shoulder and prayed.

I started going on a weekly basis. I was still drinking, but it had been reduced to a shot here and there and an occasional beer. Jim said I was suffering from anxiety. I was always amped up when I got there, so it made sense. I started listening to relaxation tapes and pretty much, just cold turkey, stopped living the life I had been. I even got a dog and named her Pearl. She was a cute six-month-old yellow lab with a black nose and the cutest eyes I had ever seen. She always greeted me with a smile and a wagging tail. I could feel myself changing. I was praying a bit, even when I was getting ready to eat. I was starting to see the world from different eyes. I had been through so much, and had seen plenty, that I think my heart was hardened from all the misery.

# CHAPTER 17

# REFLECTING

*But one thing I do: Forgetting what is behind and*
*straining toward what is ahead.*

*—Philippians 3:13*

One night I was enjoying a cigar and a beer outside on my deck. I watched as the sun was going down and Pearl was engaged in a staring contest with a squirrel sitting on a low branch in a tree. In the quiet time, my mind became a river of thoughts about my past and all the people who had been in it. I began to weep openly. Pearl ran up and started licking my hands, looking up at me with a concerned sad look.

I began to remember my life in order as it had started. How I remembered much of the bad I had done as a child. I remembered my time at the altar in that hot tabernacle in Central Texas, on my knees and praying to Christ to forgive my sins. How I wished that God would have struck me dead then so I could have gone to heaven right then and there. Why would God who loves me so let me struggle through my life and see so much pain and misery? Why did He let that girl take advantage of me, not even much more than a week after I had committed my life to Him? It wasn't a test for me. I was too young to understand what I was doing. I didn't need her forcing me into seeing to her needs and setting me on a path that I would regret the rest of my life.

One incident. How could one stupid incident change my life? Somewhere in my strange thoughts as a child, I thought people only touched each other that way because they were married or in love. That incident set me on a path of confusing sex and love. I never had a good relationship with a woman because every one of them began with sex. I looked at every woman as if I knew that all she wanted was for me to touch her and have sex with her. After all, that was my first lesson; it had to be right. Not so fast. She told me not to tell anyone, so it had to be wrong.

As I drained my emotions thinking about how much that affected my life, I then started thinking about all of the people I had affected. I had cast one woman aside for another time and time again, like they were fodder for cattle. I ruined so many relationships, not only my own, but those of other families, by committing adultery with mothers and wives of other men.

I put out my cigar, went in, and lay on my bed. The tears continued flowing as the memories continued to pour out. So, much of my life I only wanted to have "fun" only to have it crashing down around me each fucking time. I remember, after Ellie, I started looking for a type. Most of the women I sought after were like her in frame—short, thin, and small breasts. Many of the women I looked for had low self-esteem. I wanted to fix them. In my own arrogance, I thought I could heal their low self-esteem through my ability to have a physical relationship and please them in a manner that made them feel good about themselves. Me! The one person who had a lower self-esteem than any of them! I wanted God to kill me, remember? I cut myself time and time again, remember?

What a joke. As I lay there, I kept repeating each episode in my head like it was a video, and I saw each relationship crumble. And I knew why. I never, ever loved myself. I hated the thought that I was walking around in this world living a lie. No one saw the real me. I hid it so carefully. There were two people who knew the real me. One who hated me (i.e., me) and one who loved me (i.e., God). Somehow, that night, I knew I had to bring the two together. I needed God in my life. I could not manage another minute in this world I was living—dog or no dog, clean or using, sane or insane—without God. I remembered the way I was taught to pray, but it was bogus. It was just going through the motions of praying. Something wasn't right.

I fell asleep just talking to God. I talked to him as I would a friend. I told him how I needed him in my life and that I couldn't do life without him. I slept well that night. I woke up, and something was different about me. Not really changed, I just felt relaxed and at ease with myself for the first time in years.

I figured what I needed was to get away again with this new found me. I started thinking about another trip. I couldn't go back to Costa Rica. It was just too painful. I had a friend who had just got back from the Dominican Republic, and I started reading everything I could about it. I looked and read about the history there, and pictures of the beaches sold me completely. What the heck! I bought a ticket and booked a hotel in the historical district of Santo Domingo, the capital, for a few days.

I couldn't wait. This trip would be different!

# CHAPTER 18

# I AM SAVED

*For you have been saved through faith. And this is not
your own doing; it is the gift of God.*

*—Ephesians 2:8*

The plane ride from Texas to Florida was bumpy the entire way.
Then from Florida to Santo Domingo, it was worse. We flew,
what seemed to me, directly into a thunderstorm while landing. I
was sick, grumpy, and smelled horrible from sweating out the ride.

I stepped off the plane and went through the ordinary hassle
of customs. When it came time to answer how long I was going to
be here, I really wasn't sure. My plane ticket back was for two weeks
later, and my hotel reservations were only for a week in Santo
Domingo. I had no plan on this trip except to do something other
than what I had been doing.

I stepped out to get a taxi and saw more lightning and rain and
heard more thunder than I ever had in my life. This trip was going
to suck if this was normal. Then the taxi ride from the airport was

a real treat. I don't even think having a gun pointed at me years ago frightened me as much as the taxi ride. People just seemed to go at their own pace as we swerved to miss motorcycles, pedestrians, trucks, and vans. It was a serpentine ride with so many different speeds that when we arrived at the hotel, I just wanted to kiss the ground.

I stayed in an older hotel in the historical district. I was looking forward to seeing some of the older cathedrals and churches, and of course, since this was the island of Hispaniola, which Christopher Columbus discovered, I couldn't wait to see his historical places. I walked up to the desk, and this very pretty young Dominican woman walked me through the process of checking in. With her mixed English and my mixed Spanish, we managed to get through it with a few laughs. I walked into my room, drank a bottle of water, and collapsed on my bed without thought of a shower. When I woke, it was already ten o'clock in the morning.

I walked outside my door, and the humidity rushed over me; I immediately broke out into a sweat. Texas had nothing on this place. I went down and ate a breakfast of eggs, bacon, and plantains and washed it down with some strong black coffee. I walked out onto the step leading out to the *calle* and took a deep breath. You have to understand, there was a street and there was a door to the hotel. No grand entrance, mind you.

"Welcome to the Dominican Republic, sir!" said the doorman with a strong Spanish accent. He was a mixed black man near the same age as me, dressed in all white and grinning like he'd eaten all of the cookies in the jar.

I said, "*Gracias y buenos dias.*" I looked across the street, and there was a white building that looked like about four stories of apartments. There were three Dominican women on the second-story balcony, hanging up laundry and carrying on a loud conversation and laughing. Next to them and a story up, there was an old man dressed in white and wearing a straw hat, leaning against the edge of the balcony, looking down at me, and smoking a cigarette. I nodded to him, and he just kept staring.

Not much else was going on. I walked up, turned the corner, and immediately saw all of the activity was here. There were street vendors, cigar shops, and other shops of all kinds. There were street cafes, and it was loud with people making the deals of the day. I walked by a painting vendor, who had the most colorful artwork I had ever seen. I was immediately approached by a man with a badge.

"You want guide? *Mira!* I have license." He kept showing me his license, so I would know he was a legit guide.

"No, gracias, senor" was all I kept saying.

He was relentless and kept following.

"Look. No *mas*. No more. I don't need a guide."

He muttered something in Spanish and walked off.

I walked into a cigar shop, and there were a couple of shifty-looking guys in there.

"You want cigar? We have best Dominican *puros*. Made here. These the real deal."

I looked around and finally bought a box of Cohibas.

One guy got up. "Follow me."

Not again. Shit! I went ahead and followed him into another part of the store.

"*Mira!* You drink the *mamajuana?*"

What the hell? He held up a big jug of what looked like strips of bark and leaves from a tree soaking in liquid of some kind.

"*Que es?* What is it?" I asked.

"*Mamajuana. Ees* (it's) *mamajuana!*" He smiled turning the jug around for me to see. "You no know the *mamajuana*? Is good for you. Here, drink." He poured a small amount into a plastic cup.

Holy shit! It was strong, and it was good. The liquid, I found out, was rum. I still didn't know what the plants were, but didn't care. I bought a jug of it, and still tasting it in my mouth, I turned and walked back to my room to drop off my goods. I hadn't been out fifteen minutes and had already become a mark for vendors.

I walked back onto the street and crossed over, avoiding eye contact with the vendors, onto Calle Las Damas (Ladies Street). I was headed to one of the Catholic churches there to take pictures. I walked about halfway down, and there was a man sitting on a burlap sack. His eyes were milky white, and he stared straight ahead, his hand held out. I stopped for a second in front of him, reaching for a couple of coins I had in my pocket.

"No, senor. No *es necesario. Tengo algo para ti,*" he said as he stared right through me.

I wondered, *What could he possibly have for me? "Para mí hombre?"* I chuckled.

In perfect English he said, "Yes, I have something for you. Listen closely. What you seek is here. Go to the end of the street and cross over. You will see an alley. Take the alley to the end. When you come to the end, there will be a path leading into a cane field. There in the center is the building you seek. This will be your last stop."

I thought, *Yep, this is where I die. In Santo Domingo, they will bury my body in the middle of a cane field, and no one will hear from me again. Sounds about right for the way I've lived my life.*

"Senor. *Dios va a caminar contigo. No temas.*" He smiled and held both of his palms toward me and started praying in Spanish.

*Last stop? God will walk with me, huh? That's what the blind man said.* So I followed his instruction and started walking. I looked back and could hear him praying, but he wasn't sitting where I left him. *Dear God. Please, no more visions.* As I got to the alley, I passed the empty people on my way to the end of the alley. Their hollow eyes followed me my entire journey. I heard their thoughts echo against my ears as they pitied another lost mortal waiting for his end in the middle of a cane field. At the end of the alley, I couldn't believe it, but there it was. A cane field in the middle of the Santo

Domingo. I took the path, and it narrowed as I got into the cane field. I stayed steady and kept walking quite a bit. The heat and the humidity were killing me, and I hadn't thought to bring a bottled water.

I felt as though I couldn't go another step. All the thoughts I had a few weeks before started all over again. I was truly a man burdened by years of sorrow, anger, pain, anguish, and fear. The fact is I began to realize that I was truly a piece of shit, and it just weighed heavily on my mind. I didn't want to live any longer as the pictures of my life continually played in my head as I walked—the years of lies, deceit, fornication, lust, theft, gluttony, and other sins I had committed against the people and my God.

I was ready for the end.

I wanted to stop and rest. I took a few more steps on the path, surrounded by nothing but sugarcane. I kept waiting for a man with a machete to finally put me out of my misery. Then there it was. Right in front of me, in the middle of a massive cane field, was a church. It was surrounded on all sides by sugar cane. The only thing that wasn't cane was wooden steps in the front of the church and the church itself.

I looked at the steps. *I guess this is it*, I thought. I wearily climbed the ten steps to the wooden door of the church. I noticed the door had a copper knocker on it. I knew it was copper because it was oxidized to a green color from lack of care. Strangely enough, I knocked on the door of the church. I had never knocked on a church door in all of my life. Slowly, the door swung open. I walked in, touched the water in the basin, touched my head, and crossed myself. I proceeded to the altar as I had done when I was a child. I heard the door slam behind me. All of the candles in the church lit in unison. I trembled a bit and knelt at the altar. I was ready.

I began praying in the order I was taught. First I thanked God for everything I had ever received. I then prayed for forgiveness for my unworthy soul. All of a sudden, I stopped. There was a strong presence all around me. I had been praying without emotion. I had been going through the motions I learned as a kid. The presence began to get stronger. I was really frightened.

At that moment, I heard a beautiful, angelic voice say, "Rise, and turn around."

To my total surprise, I saw the form of a man. It wasn't a man, mind you; it was a form of a man. I was trembling partly from fear and partly from shock.

"Do you wish to be healed?" he asked.

"Yes. Please! I can't deal with any more pain!" I screamed.

"Step forward, my son."

I stepped forward. I stared at the figure. Now a face was formed. My eyes began at his long hair, but as I looked around his forehead, I noticed scars in a crisscross fashion underneath some of the hair that hung down. I disregarded it at first. I looked at his brown eyes. There was something soothing and peaceful in his eyes. Yet there was an immense sadness and pain in the look on his face.

But that changed. He smiled. His smile was the smile that could remove anger from the world and end all wars. It was the smile that was given to babies. I could see that he was wearing a white cotton robe. But the robe was stained with blood. I knew who this was, but, like Peter, I denied it. Yes, I began to think I was really crazy.

"Please, hurry, whoever this is, and kill me," I begged.

He held his hands outward, and I saw the wounds on each wrist; I knew they were from the nails driven into them to the cross. I glanced quickly and saw the matching wounds on his feet. I looked back to the wounds on his forehead, and I could no longer deny it. This was Jesus Christ.

I dropped at his feet and immediately began crying hysterically. I hugged his legs, began kissing his feet, and could taste the blood on my lips. Finally, I started screaming, "Please, dear Lord. Please, please, I beg of you, please forgive me. I have spent a lifetime knowing what was right and have walked away. Please forgive me for my sins. Make me whole, please, dear Lord!"

He picked me up by my arms and told me to stand still. He looked into my eyes. I was ashamed. His voice was stern, but low, as he said, "You have asked me to get you out of trouble, to kill you, to heal you, but not once have you asked me to truly forgive you until now. My son, this is all I have ever wanted from you. I was ready to forgive you long ago, but you never asked." He held his hand over my heart and said, "You are forgiven. Go and sin no more."

I felt the energy flow from his hand to my heart, and I felt a river of tears flow from my eyes for what seemed like hours. My heart began to drain the evil and impurities, and he filled me with his love and forgiveness. With my energy drained, I once again fell at his feet.

He picked me up and held me in his arms. As I stood there in his arms, I was floating, weightless and without burden. I could finally see and hear all. Everything I came in with was gone. I was free forever. The empty people outside these doors have mistakenly called this the Last Stop. I smiled and thought of this as my new beginning.

# CHAPTER 19
# GRACE

*But he gives more grace. Therefore it says, "God opposes the proud, but gives grace to the humble."*

*—James 4:6*

Yes, I was a new man. I walked out of the church door, stepped into the streets of Santo Domingo, and inhaled the air as if it were my first time. Yes, there were no cane fields. I was in downtown Santo Domingo. I was really struggling with all that had just happened. As I looked up, I saw, standing outside the church door, a strange-looking creature. It was a Dominican woman with magenta-colored hair, eyes as black as obsidian and skin the color of caramel. She was looking around me as if looking for someone to come out of the church behind me. She looked at me with a puzzled look.

I smiled. "Are you looking for someone?"

She seemed frustrated. "No *Ingles. Lo siento.*"

"Ahh," I said. "*Estas buscando a alguien?*"

She told me there was a blind man in the alley who said to come to the church steps and wait for a man to come out. This man would be the one she was looking for. OK, I was a bit puzzled. This blind man seemed to be legit, but I'm not sure if I was the guy she was looking for.

"*Tu eres* Americano?" she asked?

I told her, yes, I was an American. She quickly apologized again and said she didn't think I was the person she was to meet. I told her in my best Spanish that I was dying of thirst and was getting hungry. I asked her if she would go across the street to a street café and have a meal with me while she waited. She would be able to see the door in case the man she met came out. She looked at the door, looked at me, and back at the door. She looked at her watch, smiled, and said OK.

She was about five foot seven with a medium build. I couldn't get past the magenta hair, but when she smiled, it was sincere and full of teeth. She had a full, real smile. But I had just given my life over to Christ and realized that in my heart. I didn't have the lustful feelings of before. I looked at her as she was, a woman. She was attractive, but I left it at that. I ordered a couple of bottled waters, and she kept looking at the church. But no one came out. She asked me if I had seen anyone else in there. I told her there was not another human in there, but I did see Christ.

"Cristo?" she asked. "*En la cruz?*"

No, I told her. Not the Christ on the cross, but Christ in person. I tried in my best Spanish to tell her my story. She looked at me like I was crazy, but at least she was interested.

"OK, *esperas por favor!*" I said.

I was ready to change the conversation. I told her my name was Ram, and she told me her name was Gracia. To the best of my Spanish translation, her name was Grace.

"OK, OK, *un momento por favor,*" I said. I kind of scared her when I stopped her that suddenly. "*Su nombre es Gracia?*" I asked her.

She told me, yes, that Grace was her name.

That was it. I knew this was the time, the place, and the person who God wanted for me. I told her, "*Gracia, sé que esto suena loco, pero yo soy ese hombre que busca.*" Yes, as crazy as it sounded, my dear Grace, I was the man you were looking for.

"*Sí, lo sé,*" she answered.

She knew I was the man she was looking for. She told me she knew but wanted to make sure that I knew as well. She wanted me to realize that it was God who brought us to the same spot, at the same time, to meet each other. I had tears in my eyes.

"No, Ram. No *llores. Está bien, ya que es de Dios.*"

"Yes, Gracia. It is OK because it is from God." I understood her clearly.

We ate together and laughed as we tried to carry on a part-Spanish, part-English conversation. But as we looked into each other's eyes, we knew this was it. All of our lives spent looking, longing, and making mistake after mistake culminated to this one moment of finally meeting the one true love of our life. Yes, this was from God, Grace.

I spent the next few days getting to know Grace. We traveled to Punta Cana and hung out at the beach all day. It was more beautiful, more breathtaking than I could have imagined. We talked about all of our lives, our mistakes, our good decisions, and we talked about the grace of God. We truly got to know each other as human beings.

The time came and I was to go back to Texas. She took me to the airport. It was there where I first tried to kiss her. We had hugged and held hands but never had kissed. I reached down and held her in my arms. I leaned in to kiss her and she stopped me. "We have plenty of time for this," she said. "Please, not just now."

I was pretty frustrated, but I remembered that if I truly was going to make changes in my life and live the life of a Christian, this was the best time to start.

We hugged, and we promised to keep in touch. And we did. We talked every day by Skype. I could see that smile every day, and we continued to know each other better. I was already planning my next trip as well. I knew she was the one, but I couldn't figure out how we were going to make that happen.

I booked a trip for later that May. I couldn't wait. Everyone at work noticed the new me. I didn't go out with the folks much and had gotten involved in a Nazarene church where I was. I began a relationship with God, and I truly wanted to be the man He wanted me to be. I really worked hard at it.

One night it happened. I had a recurring nightmare. They had not been frequent as of late, and I was glad to be sleeping again. In my dream, I saw a woman riding a black horse. She was naked with long flowing black hair, and her eyes were red. I called out her name, "Susannah!" She turned the horse toward me and began galloping. I saw her reach behind her and pull out a sword. Again, I screamed, "Susannah!" She got closer, and as I held out my arms for her, she reached down and cut off my head with the sword. She snatched my head by the hair in midair and galloped away laughing, mocking me, and screaming, "Susannah!"

I woke with a start and was trembling and crying. I immediately called Gracia, and she answered after a few rings. She had been sleeping. She asked me what was wrong, and I told her about the dream. She asked if I knew the woman, and I said I did. It was someone I had been with many years before. She said, "*Tenemos que orar, ahora!*" I agreed; we had to pray now. We started praying together, she in Spanish and I in English. We prayed, and we cried for God's interference in these nightmares. We finished and were saying our good nights. She looked at me and smiled. "*Te amo, Ram.*"

"*Que?*" I asked. What did she just say to me?

"I love you, Ram," she said again, in English.

I could only sit there grinning. Someone loves me. Someone loves me, and I haven't had sex with her. Someone loves me, and I haven't kissed her. Someone loves me because God…and I stopped. Because God thinks I'm finally ready to be loved. "*Te amo, Gracia. Te amo.*"

I went back down in May for a week to study Spanish in Santo Domingo. Grace and I went out every night I was there. I got to meet her family. It was wonderful seeing such a close knit group of people, and they welcomed me into their life. They were just happy to see that Gracia was happy, and I was the man who was making that happen.

One night, we were getting in the car and she grabbed my arm and stopped me at the curb. I looked into those black eyes. I knew what to do. I pulled her into my arms and I kissed her. We kissed for a few minutes. I kept my hands to myself as we just kissed. We got in the car, and I dropped her off at her house. She looked at me as if she wanted to ask me in. She said, "*No es el momento,* Ram." She was right. It still wasn't the time. We had plenty of time.

I went back to the States to start getting things in order. I prayed and prayed that God would show me what I needed to do. Gracia and I kept talking every day. We never missed a day. We continued to tell each other that we loved each other. And I never doubted it. This time, I told her I was coming in July. It was hot as could be in July, but I didn't care. I knew what I needed to do. I told her I was flying in on Tuesday, but I had made the arrangements for Sunday. I talked to her closest family members and arranged for them to meet me with Gracia at a four-star restaurant on Monday night. She didn't know why, but about ten members of her family and her were sitting at the table. I walked in, and she saw me in the doorway and started screaming, "Ram, Ram! *¿Qué estás haciendo aquí?*" What was I doing here?

I smiled as I walked up to her. I got down on one knee and held out the ring I had just bought days before in the States. "Gracia, I ask you to please be my wife."

She started crying. But these were not tears I was familiar with from a woman. Tears of happiness. Tears of joy. "Yes, yes, Ram. I will be your wife."

Everyone started clapping and screaming. To hear Dominicans celebrate is a thing you never forget. It is loud, it is happy, and it is amazing! We celebrated into the night. I went to my hotel, got on my knees, and thanked God for sparing my life for this one night.

Gracia and I were married later that October in the same church in Santo Domingo that we met at. Needless to say, waiting for her that night was everything I had imagined and more. She was wonderful, and we were so happy. My life was finally normal. I had God, and I had Gracia.

# A NEW LIFE

*And he said to him, "Truly, I say to you, today you will be with me in Paradise."*

*—Luke 23:43*

A year later, I bought a house in the Dominican Republic, out in the country near where her family lived. The lightning began, and Grace grabbed my arm. "*Vamos.* Go outside," she said in broken Spanish and English.

That's what I like about Grace. She is so unpredictable. Clad in only her nightshirt, she ran out the door and began to dance in the yard. She danced this crazy ring-around-a-rosy dance with an imaginary partner. Some people call her crazy because of that magenta hair and because she always has these invisible friends around. Me, I still think it's cute. She's not hurting anyone.

I stood on the porch in my boxers and watched her with a smile. I was in awe of this beautiful, mature woman, still willing to be a child. As it began to pour, she ran to me, grabbed my hands, and pulled me off the porch.

"*Ven a bailar conmigo!* Hurry, before the rain stops," she said with a laugh.

"Yes, Grace. I'll dance with you."

As the rain continued, we held out our arms, put our hands together, and began to dance a merry-go-round, spinning faster and laughing until we both let go and fell onto the now-soaked ground. When we got up, Grace's wet shirt clung to her breasts. She noticed me looking, and she smiled, put her arms around me, and hugged me close. We kissed for a few minutes, while the rain drenched us both. I picked her up and carried my Grace inside where we made love until we fell asleep.

It was a long road. Thank you, God, for your Grace.

# AMAZING GRACE

Amazing grace! How sweet the sound
That saved a wretch like me!
I once was lost, but now am found;
Was blind, but now I see.

'Twas grace that taught my heart to fear,
And grace my fears relieved;
How precious did that grace appear
The hour I first believed.

Through many dangers, toils, and snares,
I have already come;
'Tis grace hath brought me safe thus far,
And grace will lead me home.

The Lord has promised good to me,
His Word my hope secures;
He will my Shield and Portion be,
As long as life endures.

Yea, when this flesh and heart shall fail,
And mortal life shall cease,

I shall possess, within the veil,
A life of joy and peace.

The earth shall soon dissolve like snow,
The sun forbear to shine;
But God, who called me here below,
Will be forever mine.

When we've been there ten thousand years,
Bright shining as the sun,
We've no less days to sing God's praise
Than when we'd first begun.

# ABOUT THE AUTHOR

Robert Lewis Wilson graduated from the University of Texas with a BA degree in accounting.

An accountant by profession, Wilson has written poems and short stories since middle school. He based this novella on his own life and on the lives of people he's met over the years.

www.ingramcontent.com/pod-product-compliance
Lightning Source LLC
Chambersburg PA
CBHW071308130626
46556CB00004B/1522